The Eye in the Dark

DCI Dani Bevan #12

By

KATHERINE PATHAK

THE GARANSAY PRESS

Books by Katherine Pathak

The Imogen and Hugh Croft Mysteries:

Aoife's Chariot

The Only Survivor

Lawful Death

The Woman Who Vanished

Memorial for the Dead
(Introducing DCI Dani Bevan)

The Ghost of Marchmont Hall

Short Story collection:

The Flawed Emerald and other Stories

DCI Dani Bevan novels:

Against A Dark Sky

On A Dark Sea

A Dark Shadow Falls

Dark as Night

The Dark Fear

Girls of The Dark

Hold Hands in the Dark

Dark Remedies

Dark Origin

The Dark Isle

Dark Enough to See

The Eye in the Dark

Standalone novels:

I Trust You

This is a work of fiction. Names, characters, businesses, places, events and incidents are either the products of the author's imagination or used in a fictitious manner. Any resemblance to actual persons, living or dead, or actual events is purely coincidental.

All rights reserved. No part of this publication may be reproduced in any form or by any means - graphic, electronic, or mechanical, including photocopying, recording, taping or information storage and retrieval systems - without the prior permission in writing of the author and publishers.

The moral right of the author has been asserted.

© Katherine Pathak, 2019

#TheEyeintheDark

Edited by: The Currie Revisionists, 2019

© Cover photograph Pixabay Images

Prologue

The noise was so loud it seemed to rattle the very foundations of the building. The deafening rumble of the engine was disturbing enough, but what made the dread tingle like pins and needles down her spine, were the eerie mechanical whines and jolts of the landing gear being engaged.

Autumn Carlisle knew exactly what each of these sounds meant. She was aware of precisely which moment the pilot would pull back on the throttle and dip the nose of the aircraft for its final descent. She'd been on hundreds of flights in her career. But lying now in the centre of her double bed, the silky covers pulled up to cover her head, the noises felt as if they'd been summoned up from the pits of hell.

When the plane had finally passed over, the nerve-shredding cacophony was replaced by the soothing hum of urban life. In this part of south-west London, it was like a piece of background music that never got turned off, regardless of whether it was day or night.

Autumn slipped out of the bed and padded into the kitchenette of her spacious flat. The air was warm and sticky. She picked up a clean glass from the draining board and held it under the cold tap, gulping down the water so thirstily that a stream ran down her chin and wet the front of her nightdress.

She put down the glass on the worktop. She splayed out her hands on the dark granite beside it, breathing deeply, in and out, until she felt calm again.

Autumn had been in the flat for three months. She had wanted to be closer to Heathrow Airport for the early morning flights. The commute had begun to wear her out. The move seemed to make perfect sense, even if it felt like a throwback to her early days as an air stewardess, fresh out of college and without the experience and status she now held.

But at the same time as she'd packed up her tatty but pretty and quirky little cottage in East Sussex, Autumn's nightmares had started. Despite working on board aircraft for over a decade, her dreams were filled with lurid images of tangled metal and pierced flesh, the reek of spilling aviation fuel. She woke in tepid sweats night after night, with the horrible sensation that she had been falling and spinning out of the sky towards the hard earth lying far below. To certain death.

Autumn shuddered at the thought of these dreams. When she moved into the flat in Hillingdon, the nightmares appeared to have become reality. Her open-plan flat under the eaves of a converted Victorian villa was rocked by regular visitations of 747s and Airbuses, manoeuvring towards the nearby landing strips at Heathrow.

Until a few months previously, the noise of aircraft hadn't bothered her at all. It was a natural part of her job and signalled the pleasant excitement and anticipation of a visit to yet another exotic location. Now, Autumn cowered from the sound, burying herself under the bedclothes like a dumb animal scrabbling terrified into its subterranean den at the sound of an unexpectedly loud noise.

She had begun to hate herself for this pitiful display of weakness. Autumn was scrupulously considerate to passengers whose fear of flying made them uncomfortable during take-off or landing, or whilst experiencing a particularly bad phase of turbulence. But behind the soothing words and reassuring gestures, she'd always felt a certain distaste for them. These people weren't strong and resilient like she was. Her top lip would curl an imperceptible fraction at the thought that their vulnerability might be contagious. Then, all of a sudden, Autumn found herself as fragile as they were. Perhaps she'd been right, it was contagious after all.

Her last trip was a short haul to Amsterdam, with an overnight stay in a hotel. She had good friends in the city. It would usually have been a job she'd look forward too. But the moment she'd entered the cabin, the sweat had pooled at the base of her spine. She was acutely aware an unsightly sheen was settling on top of her immaculately applied foundation; threatening to streak her expensive mascara and eyeliner.

Passengers expected their flight crew to exude confidence and assuredness from every pore. When the doors slid closed and the pilot fired the engines, Autumn could feel her body tensing up. It took all her strength to prevent her hands from shaking. It wouldn't be long before her fellow crew members noticed the change in her and then the passengers themselves. When that happened, she knew she was finished.

*

The next time Autumn woke, a soft grey light was filtering through her blinds. She could hear the rumble of the traffic on the main road outside, but nothing more menacing than that. It hadn't been another low-flying aircraft that had disturbed her sleep.

She glanced at the digits on her bedside clock. It was nearly 5am. The alarm would be going off soon anyway. She kicked off the thin sheets and swung her feet round to settle on the wooden floor. The coolness that seeped into her toes from the newly fitted parquet was calming.

Autumn ran the shower in her en-suite and moved back into the bedroom to lay her uniform on the bed, waiting for the water to warm up. She always dressed carefully for work. Her appearance was an important part of her role as cabin crew. You needed to be easy on the eye. She took her time selecting a matching set of lace underwear, reckoning the shower would take ages to heat up anyway. The building may have been fully refurbished within the last year, but the plumbing was still an antiquated nightmare. The water never seemed to be properly hot.

Autumn was about to slip her nightdress over her head and brave the lukewarm flow when she sensed a movement in her peripheral vision.

She remained absolutely still.

After months of battling anxiety which appeared to have no real cause, in the face of what may have been genuine danger, Autumn found herself oddly calm.

She spun round and addressed the shadows in the corner of the room, where the eaves dipped lowest. "Who are you? What do you want? Why are you watching me?"

There was no reply.

Autumn was about to reach for the main light switch when the blare of a jet engine passing directly overhead made her automatically put her hands up to cover her ears. She closed her eyes tight shut. The roar reached its peak; a crescendo of pure noise. Autumn didn't even resist as a pair of gloved hands encircled her and dragged her across the bedroom floor, into the shower cubicle; the heavy footfalls masked by the din of the low-flying aircraft.

And when she felt the sharp cut of the blade, slicing her wrists to the bone, Autumn experienced a moment of intense relief. The terrible noise had finally ceased. She heard nothing after the brief rush of pain except an oddly welcome and absolutely total, silence.

Chapter 1

Dani Bevan was enjoying the sensation of the sun warming her skin. She had her eyes closed but was not asleep. A paperback novel was resting in her lap. The sounds of suburban Glasgow on a Sunday morning were buzzing all around her, but in her own little bubble, she felt amazingly at peace.

She could hear James moving around on the patio, awkwardly shifting the heavy base of the parasol. The detective didn't open her eyes. The garden chair next to her creaked as he finally settled his weight into it. A warm hand covered her own. She smiled to herself. The soft crack of a paper spine signalled that he had opened his book.

Dani must have dropped off. When she opened her eyes again, James's book was placed on the table in front of her and the man himself was standing just inside the patio doors with the phone in his hand.

"Darling, it's for you."

She levered herself up. "I knew it was too bloody good to be true," she muttered darkly.

"It isn't work," James added encouragingly. "It's Rhodri Morgan."

Dani furrowed her brow. She'd not heard from her psychologist friend for weeks. She hoped it was a social call and nothing was wrong. She got to her feet and accepted the receiver from James's outstretched hand.

"Rhodri! How are you?" Her tone indicated she was genuinely interested.

"Hello, Danielle. I'm very well, thank you. Retirement is suiting me down to the ground."

"I'm glad to hear it. But I bet you've still got a long list of private clients."

Professor Morgan was a criminal psychologist who had worked with both the victims and perpetrators of crime for many years. Now that he had stepped down from his teaching role at the Clydebank University, he was concentrating on his private practice work. "Yes, I still have a core base of clients. But there are now a good few who I feel are ready to face the world without our sessions. It's time for them to stand on their own two feet. Besides, I may not be around forever. The time has come to wean them off, as it were."

Dani detected a maudlin note to his words. "Are you sure everything is alright, Rhodri?"

"Well, I did receive some bad news, but I'm reluctant to burden you with it. I know how busy you are."

Dani glanced wistfully in the direction of their small courtyard garden, where the twin loungers had been positioned to take best advantage of a rare display of Glasgow sunshine. She sighed inwardly. "Actually, I've got a day off, so if you wanted to meet for lunch, we could have a proper chat?"

*

Despite the warmth of the day, there were very few people sitting at the outside tables of the restaurant. Dani was determined to catch a few precious rays before the clouds moved in to cover the sun once more.

Today was the first chance the detective had had to experience this unusual spell of sunny weather. She led Rhodri straight to a seat with a view of the river, slipping off her cardigan before her friend had a chance to object.

The professor gazed at the sunshine glinting on the water. "What a lovely day," he commented in surprise, as if the heatwave which had enveloped most of Scotland for the previous fortnight hadn't until now registered in his consciousness.

"Yes, it is. The sunshine doesn't appear to bring out the best in all of us. We've had a huge upswing in reported violence, particularly between drunks at chucking out time."

Rhodri nodded. "It's a well-documented phenomenon. Historically, hot summers are often accompanied by rioting and violence."

"But *why*?" Dani shook her bob of dark brown hair in bafflement. "Surely the warm weather would put folk in a better mood?"

Rhodri chuckled. "Human nature is a fickle beast. In fact, the heat only seems to stir up our more basic instincts. It may be as simple as the longer days giving people a greater chance to drink alcohol, take drugs and mix together socially. Clashes will inevitably follow."

Dani sipped her sour lemonade, which matched her developing mood. "I should be wishing for the rain back then."

Rhodri smiled. "It's certainly what we are all more used to."

She shuffled forward. "Tell me why you wanted to meet? You said there was something on your mind?"

Rhodri sat back and sighed. "I had a phone call from an old friend a couple of weeks back. Mike Carlisle was a fellow lecturer at the university. He too retired from the job recently. He and his wife received some terrible news. Their daughter, who was working as an air hostess down in London, was found in her flat by one of the neighbours. She'd slit her wrists in the shower."

Dani shook her head sadly. "It's an awful thing to happen. How old was she?"

"Autumn Carlisle was 29 years old. She'd not married yet and seemed dedicated to her career." Rhodri furrowed his brow. "This was the reason Mike called me. He and Betsy haven't been able to accept that their daughter would take her own life. She'd just accepted a job as cabin crew supervisor at Lomond Airlines, after more than a decade at BA. Autumn had been very excited about the opportunity."

"Where do Mr and Mrs Carlisle live?"

"They have a house in Cumbernauld. But they spoke with their daughter on a weekly basis."

Dani felt a surge of pity for this couple. "Autumn was a long way from her parents and a grown woman. It's not always possible to understand what goes on in another person's head, even our closest loved ones. *We* should know that better than most."

Rhodri ignored the reference. He leant forward, his elbows resting on the table, causing the coffee to slop out of his cup. "That isn't all. The neighbour let herself into Autumn's flat because she'd heard the shower running upstairs for over an hour. She presumed Autumn had gone to work and left it on by mistake. She discovered her slumped awkwardly in the shower tray, the razor circling the plug hole and most of the blood long washed away. It struck me as an odd way for Autumn to go about it."

"Were there any prints found on the razor?"

"No, it was assumed the water had washed it clean."

Dani narrowed her eyes, her suspicions piqued. "Any sign the flat had been broken into?"

Rhodri shook his head. "But the building was a Victorian conversion with the original windows still in place. It wasn't as secure as a modern block would be." He passed a hand through his bushy grey hair. "The really odd thing was that Autumn had laid her work clothes neatly on the bed, ready for her shift that morning, even down to her matching underwear. Betsy and Mike simply can't comprehend why she would do that if she intended to end her life?"

Dani gulped the last of her lemonade. "That is an anomaly, I admit, but if Autumn had been considering suicide for some time, she may not have been thinking straight."

"I've some considerable experience of the suicidal, Danielle. That is why Mike called for my advice. I told him that Autumn's organised behaviour was unusual for someone about to take their own life. That remains my clinical opinion."

Dani realised her friend was unlikely to let this go. "Was there a suicide note?"

"No, and that's another reason to doubt the assumption. A person like Autumn, who was organised enough to lay out her clothes so precisely, would undoubtedly have left a note for her poor parents, with whom she had very good relations."

Dani considered this. As a detective, she knew relationships within families could be complicated. Rhodri only had the word of his friends that relations had been good with their daughter. It was her job to be more cynical. More detached. They may have argued in the days before her death, there could have been tensions over Autumn living so far away.

These possibilities would all have to be investigated. She also wondered if someone from the millennial generation would really write a suicide note. This wasn't the age of Agatha Christie. Perhaps the police would be more likely to find a digital message somewhere in the woman's social media accounts. Pen and paper weren't really a thing for people under 30 years of age. "If you find out from the Carlisles who the investigating officer is, I will give them a call, find out more details. That's really the best I can do."

Rhodri's worn features cracked into a relieved smile. "Thank you, Danielle. They will very much appreciate it."

Chapter 2

A hush had fallen over the department for serious crime at Police Scotland's Pitt Street headquarters. DCI Dani Bevan had gathered her team into a semi-circle in front of her office. She stood side-by-side with a tall man in his late thirties. He possessed a smooth face and a flick of dark brown hair, worn just a fraction longer than Dani would have liked.

"I want to introduce, Detective Inspector Dermot Muir," Dani began.

A chorus of muted greetings chimed around the room.

"Dermot joins us from the Royal and Diplomatic unit. He will be working with us until Alice returns from maternity leave." She paused and nodded in the man's direction. "We are very lucky to have an officer of Dermot's experience and specialist training joining our team. He has a first-class Classics degree from Oxford to his name."

Muir shifted from one foot to the other, clearly uncomfortable with his academic prowess being announced so publicly. "Thank you, Ma'am. I'm looking forward to meeting everyone."

Dani turned back to the assembled group. "There will be drinks in the boardroom at 5 o'clock this afternoon. The DCS is opening a bottle of sparkling to welcome Dermot to the department. I'll see you all there later. For now, it's back to work folks."

DS Andy Calder watched his boss lead the new recruit to the desk by the window which had previously belonged to both Phil Boag and Alice Mann. He grunted, "and guess why boyo has been singled out for the red-carpet treatment by the

DCS?"

DS Sharon Moffett, who sat opposite, cracked a weary smile. "Watch out Andy, that chip on your shoulder is showing again. Do you want salt and vinegar on it?"

Andy raised his hands in mock exasperation. "Come on, I've never known DCS Douglas to crack open the bubbly for an officer covering a maternity leave before. Of course, if that officer happens to be an Oxford graduate, well, hell, let's lay on a finger buffet while we're at it!"

Sharon chuckled. She knew Andy's inverted snobbery and hostility to career police officers tended to skew his judgement on occasion, but in this instance, she felt he had a point. Her transfer from City and Borders a couple of years before hadn't warranted anything more extravagant than a box of doughnuts from the all-night store on the corner of Pitt Street. She frowned. "Alice had better watch she doesn't stay away too long."

"*Precisely*," Andy added with considerable feeling.

Sharon couldn't ignore the irony. Not so long ago, it was DI Alice Mann who Andy considered to be the overly-educated cuckoo in the nest.

Dani noticed how Sharon and Andy had their heads bent together, their voices lowered in a muttered conversation. She'd known Calder long enough to recognise the danger signs. After logging Muir onto the system, she headed purposefully towards their workstation. "Andy, any progress on the unexplained deaths at the hotel in Trongate?"

Calder shifted up in his seat. "The next-of-kin have been notified, Ma'am. We are just awaiting the results of the *post mortems* now. We were lucky the family didn't demand their bodies be flown home. Sharon has taken witness statements from some of their fellow guests."

Dani turned to the DS, who had pulled her corkscrew curls back into a tight bun. "Did the witnesses say anything useful, Sharon?"

"Only that the Bauers had eaten in the hotel restaurant the evening before they died. I've sent the SOCOs into the kitchens to check for traces of E coli and the like."

Dani nodded. "Dermot is going to take charge of the case. He's getting himself up-to-speed right now. Carry on with what you're doing for the time-being, but you'll take your orders from him in future. Okay?"

The officers both nodded obediently, but Dani noticed the meaningful looks they flashed one another as she spun on her heels and returned to her office. She didn't have time to deal with any nonsense now. They'd simply have to get used to the new status quo, and fast.

*

Dani completed her paperwork before flicking Rhodri Morgan's email message onto the screen of her phone. The Carlisles had been prompt in providing the name of the officer in the Metropolitan Police who had handled their daughter's death.

She sighed heavily before calling the switchboard to request his office number. She had it jotted down on the notebook in front of her in minutes.

It was late in the afternoon, and Dani hoped this would mean the man would be at his desk.

The line buzzed only momentarily before it was answered. "DI Lawrence," a voice at the other end barked.

"DI Nathan Lawrence? This is DCI Dani Bevan from Police Scotland. I've got a couple of questions to ask, if I may."

"Certainly, Ma'am. What can I assist you with?"

His tone sounded uncertain. She'd clearly taken him by surprise. "I've been contacted by the parents of Autumn Carlisle, the woman found dead in her flat in Hillingdon." She felt this explanation was close enough to the truth to suffice. "They've asked me to double-check a few issues related to the investigation."

Lawrence let out an audible sigh. "I thought they might go over my head. I could tell Mr Carlisle wasn't satisfied with our conclusions."

"I have no intention of treading on your toes, DI Lawrence. But it's a difficult situation. The couple have lost their daughter and had no clue she was suicidal. They just want to be certain, that's all."

"Well, as you know, Ma'am, that isn't always possible. But fire away, what are the couple concerned about specifically?"

"There were no prints found on the razor. Did your techies think it could have been wiped?"

"They said it was possible, but more likely, any prints were washed away by the water from the shower, which was running for approximately one hour after Autumn's time of death."

Dani made a note. "And the clothes which had been laid neatly on the bed. Our consultant psychologist suggests this behaviour was too organised for someone about to kill themselves in such a violent way."

There was a pause on the line, before the officer replied, "I did find that odd, I must admit. But again, we consulted with the shrink on our own books. She said it would fit with Autumn being a very organised and methodical person. Cutting her wrists in the running water meant the scene would be clean for anyone finding her. It indicated a clinical, ordered approach to the suicide, matched by the clothes being so neatly presented."

Dani crinkled her brow. "Surely by that logic, Autumn would have never left anything out on the bed at all. She wouldn't have wanted to leave any loose ends behind her. And there was no suicide note. It seems she was close to her parents, they spoke every week. It doesn't make sense. A highly organised personality would surely have written a note. Did you find anything on her computer or phone?"

The DI was clearly working hard to keep the frustration out of his tone. "There were no unusual messages on her social media accounts. But there was also no sign of a break-in at the flat. No prints other than those belonging to the victim were discovered in that bedroom. The place had been fully re-furbished before she moved in and the neighbours swear there'd not been a single visitor since."

"But this is London we're talking about. Do people really notice the comings and goings of their neighbours?" Dani hadn't intended to be so argumentative, but the man's stubborn attitude was managing to wind her up. "Have her friends and work colleagues been questioned? I'd like to take a look at the transcripts of the interviews."

"Of course, Ma'am. I'll have them emailed over to you by first thing tomorrow morning. Now, if there's nothing more, I've got work to do."

Before Dani could respond, the line went dead. She stared at the receiver for a full minute before replacing it with some force. "What an arsehole," she muttered to herself, before shaking the encounter from her mind and checking the clock that hung over the door. It was gone five o'clock, time to head to the boardroom before the DCS cracked open the bubbly without her.

Chapter 3

Sharon had clipped her unruly curls back from her plump, rosy face for her visit to the kitchens of the Berkley Hotel. The DS wanted to avoid being forced to wear one of those hats that resembled a shower cap. Andy would never stop ripping the piss if she did. It wouldn't be beyond him to take a picture of her in it on his phone and plaster printouts all over the noticeboard. She couldn't take the risk.

As it happened, the hotel manager, Mr Bartlett, steered her away from the service area to a salubrious ground floor office instead.

"Please take a seat, Detective Sergeant. I can have some afternoon tea brought in for us?" The man was tall and impeccably dressed in an expensive, tailored suit.

"That won't be necessary, Sir. I just want to run through our forensic results with you." Sharon perched her ample weight on the arm of a velvet sofa. She flipped open her tablet.

The manager paled. "Do I need to contact our lawyer?"

Sharon's expression softened. "Let's discuss the details first."

He pulled up a chair and folded himself into it. "Go ahead."

"Firstly, the results from the examination of your kitchens indicated no evidence of food poison toxins on the worktops or the leftover items in the bins. In fact, our SOCOs think you well deserve your 5-star hygiene rating. In addition to this, no other guests who ate in the dining room on the evening of the 28th have experienced any health problems."

The manager shifted up in his seat. "Well, that's good to hear."

Sharon held up her hand. "But the *post mortem* results weren't quite so conclusive. Both Mr and Mrs Bauer had mild heart complaints, for which they took medicine prescribed for them back in Frankfurt. It seems they both suffered congestive heart failure during the night. There was evidence of moderate alcohol consumption in both victims which would have taken place in the 12 hours before, but not enough to explain their deaths." Sharon leant forward. "In brief, the *PM*s were inconclusive as to cause of death. Our pathologist says it is extremely uncommon for two people to die in their sleep within hours of one another in the same bed without some outside cause. But to be honest, Sir, at this point in time we can't find one."

The hotel manager's posture slumped. "I am very sorry for Mr and Mrs Bauer and their family, but this is also terrible news for the hotel and our entire chain. If there is no explanation, people will blame the hotel. Our owner will not be pleased."

Sharon shrugged. "We will continue our investigations, but right now, I can't provide you with any clear answers. I've got to say as much to the next-of-kin, when they arrive tomorrow."

"Yes, that will certainly be a difficult conversation." His head lifted, and a flicker of optimism danced across his lined features. "Perhaps *we* could offer the family free accommodation whilst they are here? I could set aside the premier suite for their use?"

Sharon got to her feet. "I'll pass the offer on," she replied without enthusiasm. "But something tells me they may just decide to find a different hotel."

*

James was filling the dishwasher when Dani returned home to their flat in Scotstounhill. He glanced up as she entered the kitchen.

"Sorry, darling. I wasn't expecting you back so early. I've already eaten."

Dani slid onto one of the chairs at the dining table. "Don't worry, I'll fix myself something later. I wanted to look through the evidence the Met sent me on the Autumn Carlisle case in peace."

James moved across the room and bent down to place a kiss on her lips. "The suicide that Rhodri is connected to?"

"That's right. I got the distinct impression the investigating officer did *not* appreciate my interference."

James lifted down a couple of goblets from a cupboard, filling them from a half empty wine bottle on the counter. "Well, would you like it if a superior officer from another division started questioning your findings on a case?"

Dani grunted, before taking a gulp from her glass. "Probably not. But as a DI I would have been diplomatic enough not to show it."

James slipped his arm around her shoulders. "Ah, the younger generation. They've got no manners."

Dani laughed. "He's not that much younger than us!"

"Speaking of which, how is your *wunderkind* new recruit to the department settling in?"

"Dermot? He seems very bright. I left him discussing the Berkley Hotel deaths with Sharon and Andy. I might try to hang onto him after Alice returns, we've been short-staffed for months."

"I'm sure Andy will *love* that. Oxbridge fast-trackers are just the kind of people he enjoys taking orders from." James arched his eyebrows wickedly.

Dani shrugged, reaching down to massage her stockinged foot. "He'll just have to get used to it. Dermot seems like a decent guy. If Andy wants more power over his life at Pitt Street, he should take the inspector exams himself."

"I think he enjoys heckling from the sidelines too much."

"Precisely. I like Sharon a great deal; I believe she's an excellent, intuitive detective, but I'm not sure she and Andy are a good influence on each other. When I've got more staff, I'll be able to mix them up; start pairing them with other officers."

"You sound like a schoolteacher, separating the naughty ones."

"Sometimes, managing the department feels exactly like that." Dani drained her glass and turned her attention to the pile of papers in front of her.

*

It struck Dani that DI Lawrence's officers had done a reasonably thorough job. Autumn Carlisle had only been working at Lomond Airlines for six months before her death. The Met officers interviewed her fellow cabin crew and immediate boss at Lomond, but also spoke with some of her previous colleagues at BA, where she had worked for most of her career.

The witness statements seemed to echo one another; Autumn was a capable, motivated individual who was always extremely business-like in the workplace. Her boss at Lomond had been shocked to hear of her death. He felt she'd settled in very well leading her new team. Autumn had managed the crew on a recent flight to Amsterdam which had gone perfectly smoothly, according to the written reports.

The only hint of dissension came from one of the stewardesses she was managing. Dani flicked back through the papers to take a note of her name. Kathy Brice. She had told the Met officer who interviewed her that Autumn had been jumpy on that flight to Amsterdam; constantly mopping beads of sweat from her face, despite the temperature-controlled environment. Her boss had been short in response to passengers' requests. She hadn't exuded her usual calm, patient persona.

Dani shuffled through the printed-out transcripts one more time. Autumn appeared to have had few friends outside of the workplace. Her parents gave the names of a few previous boyfriends, but none had been on the scene for at least a year.

James clicked on the main light as he entered the room. "You'll strain your eyes reading those documents in the dark," he admonished. "Do you want a coffee, I'm making some?"

She shook her head. "Have you ever known someone who has worked for an airline – cabin crew, I mean?"

James filled the coffee machine with beans. The kitchen was suddenly flooded with the sharp, bitter aroma. He pulled a face. "Actually, I dated an air stewardess for a while, when I was living down in London. Years ago, now."

Dani lifted her head. "Why did the relationship end?"

"Jeanette was working on the long-haul flights from Gatwick. It was difficult to match one-another's schedules. It just fizzled out. To be honest, she was very attractive, but we didn't have much in common."

"What was the appeal of the job for her, do you know?"

James ran a hand through his greying hair. "She loved the travel and meeting new people. Jeanette said she got a real buzz each time the plane took off, like anything in the world was possible. But it was a bugger if you wanted to put down roots."

Dani nodded. "I can imagine that." She moved across to put her arms around him. "I expect it could be a lonely life too. Autumn must have spent hundreds of nights alone in hotel rooms."

James nuzzled her cheek. "Maybe she wasn't alone," he muttered in her ear.

She pulled back. "I suppose that's true. Autumn was a very attractive woman, who laid out matching lingerie to wear under her work clothes. To imagine that she was celibate simply because there was no permanent boyfriend on the scene is probably naïve."

"But does her sex life have any bearing on whether the woman committed suicide or not?"

Dani sighed heavily. "Without more information, I really couldn't say."

"Then let's call it a night." He twisted a stray lock of her hair between his fingers.

"Sure," she said resignedly. "I can call Rhodri in the morning."

Chapter 4

Dermot Muir had organised his work station just as he wanted it. The cumbersome PCs which some of the desks still accommodated were not for him. He'd called down to tech support to have his terminal disconnected and removed within minutes of arrival.

Everything was on the cloud these days, including the Police Scotland databases. The DI wouldn't need anything other than his tablet and phone to keep up-to-date. It meant he could also write his reports from home, which would hopefully keep his girlfriend Serena happy.

She'd not been impressed with the long hours he'd worked shadowing members of the diplomatic service. It was the reason he'd taken the temporary job at the SCU; he was hoping to save his relationship.

Sharon approached his desk. "The Bauers' son has arrived in reception, boss."

He got to his feet. "Has he identified the bodies?"

She nodded. "One of the uniforms gave him a lift here after visiting the morgue."

"Have him sent to one of the interview rooms, please."

"Sure thing."

"And will you come and talk to him with me? You are the one with the greatest knowledge of the case."

"Of course. By the way, the pathologist told me he has perfect English."

"The Germans usually do."

Sharon smiled. She decided the new DI might be an okay guy after all.

*

Stefan Bauer looked to be in his mid-forties. He wore brown corduroy trousers and a cotton shirt, open at the neck. Sharon thought he appeared as shaken as she would expect someone to be after just viewing the dead bodies of both their parents.

"Would you like a tea or coffee?" Dermot began.

Stefan shook his head. "I had a drink at the mortuary. Please, I just want to know how your investigation is developing?"

Dermot sat down opposite the man. "Firstly, on behalf of my team, I'd like to convey our sincere condolences to you and your family."

Stefan nodded his acknowledgement.

Sharon could tell that Muir's time with the diplomatic service had left its mark. She briefly considered whether Calder should give it a go.

The DI continued. "I'm afraid the *post mortem* examinations did not provide us with any conclusive answers. It seems both your parents suffered heart failure during the night of the 28th June. Your mother died approximately two hours after your father. Their medical records show both suffered from angina and took medicine for it?"

"Yes, my father's heart condition was long-standing, but for our mum, it only developed in the last couple of years."

"Had they been in any unusually stressful situations recently?"

Stefan considered this. "I'll have to ask my sister, Mila. She spoke with our mother most days. But I would have to say no. They have lived in their house in Frankfurt for over twenty years. Father retired eight years ago. They were taking a trip to Scotland to see the sights. Their sudden deaths have no explanation for us."

"I can understand the situation is frustrating," Sharon interjected. "I have visited the hotel where Mr and Mrs Bauer were staying. The room has been thoroughly examined and the staff questioned. There was no trace of food poisoning in the kitchens, or emissions of carbon monoxide in the room. I realise that your parents dying within hours of one another is highly unusual, but these odd occurrences do happen."

Stefan's brown eyes began to pool with tears. "I want to see the room, the place where they died."

Sharon glanced at her colleague. "Yes, we can arrange that."

Stefan swept a hand across his face, clearly not willing to express his emotions in front of the detectives. "Mila and I have been reading the press coverage of our parents' deaths here in your papers. Some journalists are speculating that our parents were killed by some kind of untraceable *nerve agent*. They are saying maybe my father was an informant for the West when he was still working as a scientist for the old GDR. It has upset my family a great deal."

Dermot raised his hand. "It is extremely regrettable that some of the newspapers have seen fit to take this line. With the attack on the Skripals in Salisbury earlier this year, there have been some unhelpful comparisons drawn with your parents' situation; being foreign nationals dying in unexplained circumstances. But let me be clear, there was absolutely no trace of any such substance present in your parents when they died. If there were, the hotel would have been quarantined immediately."

"Yes, yes, I know this. It is a ridiculous story. My father began his career in a government-controlled research lab in East Germany. When the wall came down, he moved to a private company in Frankfurt.

Many others did the same after re-unification. It is not a crime. And it certainly does not mean he was a *spy*."

"No, of course it doesn't," Sharon soothed. "I recommend that you try to avoid reading the newspaper reports. It will only be upsetting for your family. It is best to liaise only with us. The circumstances of your parents' deaths are unusual and will attract press attention. Without any solid answers there will be mis-information. It's better to steer clear."

Stefan leant forward, placing his hands on the table. "Mila and I are looking for answers too. It seems even the police cannot provide them."

Dermot assumed a conciliatory tone. "We will arrange for you and your sister to visit the Berkley Hotel this afternoon. Do you have a mobile number we can reach you on?"

Stefan rooted in his trouser pocket for his phone. "Thank you, DI Muir. We would appreciate being allowed to visit the place our parents died. Because I can assure you, we will not be returning to Germany until we know more about what happened to them."

Chapter 5

The couple seated on the leather sofa in Rhodri Morgan's high-ceilinged sitting room looked lost and diminished amongst their surroundings.

Dani pulled her seat closer to them. "Mr and Mrs Carlisle, I'm very sorry for your loss."

The lady dipped her head sadly. "Thank you for your kind words. Please call us Betsy and Mike."

Rhodri entered with a tray of coffees. "The detective chief inspector has spoken with the Metropolitan Police," he declared, doling out the china cups.

Betsy Carlisle was a neat, attractive woman with waved hair that was dyed a deep chestnut colour. Her husband was taller but with a thin frame. His face was healthily tanned but gaunt and slack with grief.

"Thank you for taking the time to do that," Mike commented. "We really didn't want to make a fuss, but still, the situation felt extremely unsatisfactory."

Dani had a sudden and strong urge to help this couple who, 'didn't want to make a fuss'. In her experience, they were usually the people with the greatest cause for complaint. "I spoke with DI Lawrence. He supplied me with their forensic analyses and witness statements." She sipped her coffee. "I can see why they came to the conclusions they did."

"Yes, on the surface, the evidence seems to suggest that Autumn took her own life," Betsy stated. "But I'd spoken with her only days before. Our daughter was full of plans for her future at Lomond Airlines. She'd only been in the new job for a few months. Autumn was such a determined, focused person."

Rhodri adopted a kindly tone. "People can change, Betsy, especially if they have been experiencing a mental health crisis. Autumn may not have shared her innermost feelings with you."

Mike put down his cup. "Actually, she *had* shared something with us, the last time she was visiting in Cumberbauld."

Betsy shot him a warning glance. "We weren't going to mention *that*."

Mike shrugged. "If the detective inspector is giving up her time to help us, she deserves to know everything."

Dani nodded encouragingly. "Anything you can tell me about your daughter would be of assistance."

The man sighed heavily. "Autumn stayed with us for a couple of nights in May. I came downstairs at about 2am for a drink of water and found her sitting on the sofa with a book. I asked what was wrong. She told me that she'd been having difficulty sleeping. It'd been going on since she'd moved out of her old cottage."

Betsy clasped her husband's hand. "It was most unusual for her. Autumn was always a good sleeper, she was the same as a baby. Out like a light without a care in the world. She was born on a beautiful October day; her wisps of auburn hair matched the leaves that covered the grounds of the hospital. It's the reason we gave her the name."

Mike smiled at his wife tolerantly. "She'd been suffering from nightmares. I made her a mug of warm milk and she described the dreams to me."

Rhodri was listening with interest.

"Autumn would wake in the middle of the night with her heart racing. Sometimes she had dreamt of plane crashes and of falling from the sky, but most often, she saw a glowing eye watching her from out of the darkness. This disturbed her the most."

"What did she mean by an 'eye'?" Rhodri asked keenly, knowing that dreams could be full of symbols from deep within the psyche.

Mike shook his head in frustration. "I didn't question her enough about it. I was trying to persuade her that it was just a phase, it would pass. I suppose I was trying to downplay the whole thing."

"They sound like typical anxiety dreams," Dani added. "Your daughter had recently moved home and started a new job, one with management responsibilities. Her disturbed sleep could simply have reflected the stress she'd been under."

"Was that enough to cause her to do what she did? People change jobs all the time and move house, it's possible to cope with that, isn't it?" Betsy was ringing a handkerchief in her lap, her tone agitated.

"For what it's worth, Betsy, there were a few details that left me dissatisfied with the verdict of the police. I'm going to contact the Medical Examiner and ask him to delay the inquest whilst I look into the case further."

Mike rose to his feet. "*Really?* I can't thank you enough, DCI Bevan."

"Please don't raise your hopes. It's unlikely I'm going to find any drastically new evidence."

"No, but Rhodri thinks very highly of you. If you look into things and discover that Autumn *did* take her own life, we will be prepared to accept it."

Dani sipped her coffee slowly. She hoped the faith this couple seemed to have in her would not prove to be misplaced.

*

Dermot Muir took the upright chair in Dani's office, whilst Andy and Sharon perched next to each other on the tiny sofa, their knees nearly up to their chests, like little children.

Dani flipped through the file of notes. "Stefan Bauer mentioned his father used to work for the East German government, back when it was Soviet controlled, before communism collapsed in 1990 and Germany re-unified. Do we know what kind of work he actually did?"

Sharon raised her head. "He was working as a Biochemist for a pharmaceutical company in Frankfurt before he retired. To be honest, I've no idea what he did before that. I'd have to contact some people in Germany to find out more. I didn't think it would be relevant, Ma'am. There's no evidence to suggest the Bauers' deaths were deliberate. His past life didn't seem important."

Dani crinkled her brow. "Well, the press seems to have been exploring this angle. I wouldn't like to think we were missing a trick."

Dermot cut in, "it appears some journalists are determined to make a connection between these deaths and the nerve agent attack in Salisbury. There have been hints that some special poison was used which leaves no traces. It's pure fantasy." He cleared his throat. "I called one of my contacts in the intelligence service. I worked with their officers in my role at the Diplomatic Branch."

Andy rolled his eyes.

"They had no record of either Greta or Klaus Bauer ever having worked for the Stasi or having provided information to the British or US secret services."

Dani nodded. She was impressed. "Then are we ready to pass the documents over to the Procurator Fiscal's Office, for them to reach their final verdict?"

"I'd say so, Ma'am," Sharon said with confidence. "Andy and I took Stefan and Mila Bauer to view the room where their parents died. They both cried a bit and the hotel manager gave them tea in the lounge. I believe they were placated by the visit."

"Okay," Dani crossed her arms over her chest. "Looks like we're ready to sign this one off."

The officers stood, recognising the signal to return to their desks.

"Andy, can you stay behind a moment?"

Sharon and Dermot swept from the room, closing the door behind them.

Andy dropped into the chair in front of his boss. "Is anything wrong, Ma'am?"

"No, I just wanted an update on how Dermot was slotting in."

Andy smirked. "Fine, actually. Even if he does think he's James Bond."

"His experience with the diplomatic unit could prove very useful to us. He's bringing a new set of skills to the table."

"I suppose so." Andy's posture slouched, like a recalcitrant teenager.

"I want you to do your best to welcome Dermot into the team."

"But he's only temporary, Ma'am. Alice will be back in a few months."

"We've been short-staffed since Phil left. If I can keep Dermot *and* Alice, it would be the perfect scenario for the SCU. We'd all benefit from a lighter workload."

Andy was on his feet. "Certainly, Ma'am. I'll do my best."

Dani watched her old friend lumber back to his workstation and sling his jacket over the back of his chair. She wondered if he'd taken any notice of her request at all.

Chapter 6

Warm rain was pounding the pavement as Dani approached the entrance to the police station on Hammersmith Road in London. She sat in her damp suit in a side room off the reception area for a full half an hour before anyone came to greet her.

When a tall, good-looking man in his mid-thirties threw open the door, the DCI tried to hide her irritation at the delay.

He extended one of his rangy arms. "You must be DCI Bevan, pleased to meet you. DI Nathan Lawrence."

"Call me Dani, please." She returned his surprisingly warm handshake.

"Likewise, I'm known as Nate. No point in standing on ceremony."

Dani followed him along a corridor and up a flight of stairs to the floor which she assumed housed the criminal investigation unit. Nate weaved between the rows of desks until he found his own, dragging out a chair for her to sit on.

"You've come a long way, Dani. I hope this won't be a wasted trip for you." Nate leant back in his seat, appraising his visitor with piercing blue eyes. His expression was friendly, but the DCI still got the faint impression he was mocking her.

"I'd like to view Autumn Carlisle's flat, if that's possible, and if I could take a look at her laptop and personal effects that would be helpful too?"

"Sure. We've got them bagged up in the evidence room downstairs. One of the DCs, Trudy Gifford, analysed the computer and phone. I'll introduce you." He examined her face for a moment. "What did you say your connection was to this case again? It's got a personal angle, right?"

Dani endeavoured to shake her sense that the detective's manner was abrasive. "There is a psychologist back in Glasgow who I have liaised with on a number of cases. He is friends with Autumn Carlisle's parents. He doesn't feel the evidence suggests suicide. I have learnt to take his opinion very seriously. He was the practitioner who helped to resolve the Ian Cummings' murders, from back in the eighties. We worked closely with the Met over that. The results were widely publicised. It was quite a coup for the force."

Nate shrugged his broad shoulders, clearing his throat awkwardly. "I did read about it, yes. But with respect, Ma'am, I've never come across an intervention like this in an active investigation before, not from another division so far away, certainly." He met her eyes with his steely gaze once again. "But what the hell, we all want to get to the truth, don't we?"

Dani nodded, not trusting herself to reply. She needed this man on side if she was going to get the kind of access to the evidence that she wanted.

Nate stood, gesticulating to a middle-aged woman who sat a couple of desks down. "Hey, Trudy! Can you spend an hour or so with Dani here? She wants the lowdown on the Carlisle laptop data."

"Of course," the woman replied cheerfully.

Dani got to her feet too, retreating from the vicinity of DI Lawrence as swiftly as possible.

*

The rain had stopped, but the skies remained grey over west London. Dani was driven by DC Trudy Gifford to the address of the Victorian conversion in

Hillingdon where the top floor comprised of Autumn Carlisle's flat.

As she stepped onto the pavement, Dani almost cowered as the sudden roar of a commercial aircraft exploded overhead. "Good God!" she exclaimed. "Do they always come in that low? The undercarriage practically skimmed the roof of that house!"

Trudy nodded tolerantly. "Yep, around here they do. I live just the other side of the Hammersmith Flyover. We're hoping this new runway isn't going to make our street just like this one."

Dani glanced cautiously at the skies above them. She wasn't at all sure she could live this way. But then, perhaps people got used to it. To her, it felt akin to living in a war zone.

The flat was up two flights of stairs. A cross of police tape was still securing the front door. Trudy ripped it out of the way and turned a key in the lock. "We'll be passing the place back to the landlord in a few days. He wants to get it rented out again quick. There's a high demand for these properties from workers at Heathrow."

Dani stepped into a narrow corridor with stripped oak floorboards and Velux windows in the eaves. A small kitchen was positioned off to one side. Everything in it appeared brand new.

As if following Dani's train of thought, Trudy stated, "the flat was completely re-furbished last year. It doesn't seem as if Miss Carlisle used the kitchen much after she moved in."

"I suppose she was away a lot," Dani added, noting the occupant had put up a couple of framed photographs on the walls of the lounge area. They were mostly of exotic locations minus human life. Only one was of Autumn herself, posing on a bridge in what appeared to be Amsterdam.

"This is the important bit," Trudy explained,

leading Dani into a master bedroom with connecting en-suite, which was built into the narrowest projection of the eaves. It was immediately evident where the technicians had labelled blood splatters in the otherwise pristine bathroom.

"The clothes on the bed, the razor and night clothes were all bagged up for forensic testing. You can view those back at the station." Trudy retreated to the doorway, allowing her superior to examine the room in peace.

Dani drank in the scene. The bed had been stripped, but the mattress and divan were clearly top of the range. She flicked through the clothes hanging on the rails in the wardrobe. They were mostly designer casual wear. The drawers emitted a perfumed scent as she tugged them open and were filled with fancy underwear, which Dani noted was tasteful rather than tarty.

The DCI stood at the end of the bed, trying to imagine the thought processes that would have been running through Autumn's head as she decided not to put on the clothing she'd laid out so carefully on her expensive sheets, but instead to take a razor from a bathroom cabinet and slit her wrists, accepting that her life was over and no hope remained.

She squatted down on the floor, between the base of the bed and the entrance to the bathroom, running her hand along the smooth wood of the interlocking boards as they formed their parquet pattern. "What's this?" Her vision had been drawn to an ugly black streak across the otherwise immaculate floorboard.

Trudy stepped forward to join her, dropping down onto her haunches. "It looks like a scuff mark. It's very dark, perhaps from a black shoe? Maybe one of the deceased's?"

Dani glanced over to the wardrobe. She couldn't see any footwear lined up along the base. "Where did Autumn keep her shoes? I bet she had a pretty good collection of stilettos and the like?"

"There's a cabinet in the hallway with pull-out drawers. That's where all her shoes were kept."

Dani looked the woman in the eye. "It's not likely she wore them in the bedroom then?"

Trudy shrugged. "We can't be certain of that."

"Was this mark on the flooring photographed and catalogued by the original tech team?"

Trudy hesitated. "I don't believe so, Ma'am."

Dani got to her feet. "Then I think we'd better get that team back up here ASAP, don't you? I have to assume the SOCOs didn't compromise the scene themselves, so this mark must have been made *pre-mortem.* Have you got DI Lawrence's number on your phone?"

Trudy nodded with resignation. "I'll call him right now, Ma'am." She ran a hand through her wavy hair. "I can tell you for nothing, he won't be happy."

Dani's expression was fixed in a grim line. "Well," she added stiffly, "that will make two of us."

Chapter 7

Nate Lawrence's cheeks were flushed crimson. His dark hair was ruffled and his shirt had come loose from his trousers. Dani surmised that DI Lawrence was the type of person whose appearance tended to unravel along with their mood.

The detectives stood facing one another in the lounge of Autumn Carlisle's flat.

"How are the SOCOs supposed to ascertain whether this mark on the bedroom floor occurred on the morning of Miss Carlisle's death, or simply came from the boot of one of the workmen who fitted the bathroom, several months ago?"

"So, you also think it's a boot mark?" Dani maintained eye contact with the detective.

Lawrence shifted his weight from one foot to the other. "I'm no expert, obviously, but that's how it appears, yes." The words were delivered begrudgingly.

"In answer to your question, I believe if the scuff mark had been left by a workman, there would be more, in other parts of the flat. But there was just the one and it is positioned directly between the bed and the shower room."

Lawrence breathed in deeply, rubbing both hands through his hair, sending it up into even more unruly tufts. "But *if*, and I'm only saying *if*, there was an intruder in this flat when Autumn died, wouldn't there also have been further indications of his presence – more marks on the floorboards, an open window, *fingerprints* on the door knobs?"

"This intruder was obviously careful. They must have worn gloves and had a way to enter the flat without leaving a trace. But in order to overpower Autumn and drag her into the shower cubicle, there must have been a struggle. This was the point when the scuff mark was left."

Lawrence sighed. "It's conjecture at this point."

"Yes, but it fits with the other evidence. The clothes neatly laid out on the bed, including the underwear. No suicide note left for her devoted parents." Dani moved aside as one of the techies exited the bedroom, heading for the front door.

The DI dropped onto the arm of the small sofa. "Okay, if, as a team, we entertain the scenario of an intruder, what would you recommend we do next?"

Dani softened her tone. "You need to get the SOCOs to examine the roof for starters. I noticed an external fire escape when DC Gifford and I arrived. Our killer may have entered through one of the windows in the roof. Top floor flats can get very hot. Autumn may have left one of the Velux windows open a crack. She may have felt safer being this high up in the building, resulting in her being prepared to take this small risk. The weather has been unusually warm lately."

The DI nodded. But before he could answer, the building shook with the noise of an aircraft passing overhead. It took a couple of minutes for the cacophony to subside. "Jesus Christ!" He exclaimed. "What in merry hell was that?"

Dani tipped her head skyward. "*That* was the reason no one in the building heard the struggle between Autumn and her attacker. Those things go overhead about every hour."

Lawrence's expression was grim. "Why didn't I clock that myself?"

"Because the superficial evidence suggested suicide. That meant your tech teams weren't here long enough to notice, or to recognise the significance. You had no real reason to assume that suicide wasn't the case in this instance. I imagine there are more suicides in London than there are murders?"

"Yeah, about tenfold."

"Then you made a perfectly logical assumption that you were dealing with a suicide here."

"I used to work the river in my days as a DC. We had a bridge jumper about once a month. They never left any notes either."

"Then there you go." Dani wondered why she was wasting time massaging this man's ego. "Now, we need to get a new set of forensics off to the lab. I'd also suggest questioning the neighbours again. They may have seen someone hanging around the building in the last few weeks. The intruder must have known Autumn's movements and routine."

He jumped to his feet. "I'm on it." He eyed her cautiously. "Is there any chance you might be able to stay on here for a couple more days?"

Dani cracked a half smile. "It seems like I might have to."

*

Dani had left Nate Lawrence and his team to re-interview the neighbours in Hillingdon. The DCI had decided to pay a visit to Autumn Carlisle's place of work.

Trudy had recommended she take the Underground to Heathrow airport, suggesting the roads were too congested to bother negotiating at that time of day. Dani appreciated the local knowledge.

Lomond Airlines had an office on the top floor of one of the terminal buildings. The desks looked out on a bank of tall windows which framed the impressive fleet of planes lining the tarmac below. Dani was led to the office of the CEO of Lomond Airlines himself, Denny Lomond.

The DCI recognised the man immediately. He was one of Scotland's most successful entrepreneurs. Denny was often being interviewed on TV about topics that ranged from the expansion of his leisure empire to zero-hour contracts and the impact of Brexit.

The man wasn't as tall as he appeared on the small screen. In real life he was stocky in build, with a smooth pate, but still handsome in a tanned, rugged way. He moved out from behind his desk to shake her hand.

"Thank you for agreeing to see me at such short notice, Mr Lomond." Dani took a seat.

"My door is always open to a fellow Scot." He knitted his lined brow. "But the subject of your visit concerns me greatly. You believe the death of poor Autumn may have been murder?"

Dani was taken-aback by his directness. But then she imagined it came with the territory in his line of work. "We are still ascertaining the facts, but we have fresh evidence to suggest there was an intruder in Miss Carlisle's flat on the morning she died."

Denny whistled. "Well, I must admit I never bought into the idea of Autumn being suicidal. She seemed pretty much in control of her life to me. Hell, it's why I offered her the promotion to management."

"Autumn had been working for you this last three months?"

"That's right. I'm expanding my operation down here. As you probably know, I've been running short-haul flights out of Prestwick for years. I felt the time had come to enter the international market. So, I'm on the lookout for great staff. I've got some eyes and ears at all the big operators. I was told that Autumn was one of the best."

"This was when she worked for BA?"

"Yes, she had a great reputation there. I approached her myself to offer her a job here. It took a couple of meetings to persuade her to switch."

"You got to know her quite well, then?"

Denny shrugged his shoulders. "We had lunch and talked about the aviation industry. I wouldn't say she got to know much about me personally or vice-versa."

Dani glanced at her notes. "I'm keen to speak with her co-workers. I know they were interviewed once already, but in the light of the new evidence, I will need to speak with them again. Particularly a member of your cabin crew named Kathy Brice?"

"I'll place you in the capable hands of my PA. She'll sort that out for you, but I must warn you, some of the staff on your list may be in the air."

Dani nodded. "I expected that might be the case."

Denny leant forward. "It's a strange life they lead. It wouldn't be for me."

Dani crinkled her brow in puzzlement. "What do you mean?"

"Spending more than half of your life up there in the sky." His compact body shuddered fractionally, a shadow passing across his features. "I prefer to be on *terra-firma*. If you know what I mean?"

Dani smiled. She did know what he meant but thought it a strange thing for the aviation entrepreneur Denny Lomond to have said.

Chapter 8

When addressing his team in the incident room at Hammersmith Road Police Station, DI Lawrence appeared more professional than Dani had seen him at any point so far in their brief acquaintance.

A series of crime scene photographs were displayed on a smartboard behind him. "The scuff marks found by DCI Bevan of Police Scotland have been identified as containing traces of rubber and moulded plastic. According to the tech team, this suggests they originate from the sole of a shoe. There is no way to ascertain how fresh the marks are, but the experts suggested the stain had been there for days rather than weeks."

"How do they know that?" One of the officers enquired.

"Because the residue was lying on top of the polished floorboards. It wouldn't have taken long for natural footfall to have eroded and wiped it away. As the DCI so astutely pointed out, the mark lay in the direct path that our victim would have taken from her bed to the en-suite. Even with bare feet passing over it, the mark would have been gone in a few days."

Trudy raised her hand. "So, are we now assuming that Autumn Carlisle was a *victim* of a violent attack at the hands of an intruder?"

Lawrence opened his wide arms in a gesture of supplication. "We are now treating the death of Autumn Carlisle as suspicious. I'll hold my hands up to it folks. So far, I've royally cocked up. Somehow, we missed this piece of vital evidence first time around."

Dani stepped forward, not wanting the briefing to turn into an outlet for Nate Lawrence to vent his remorse. "It's very common in the early stages of an investigation for a piece of evidence like this to be missed. The scuff mark may yet turn out to indicate nothing, but it does mean that murder has become a real possibility." She glanced at the DI, who appeared happy to let her speak. "Yesterday, I called in on the offices of Lomond Airlines, where Autumn worked. Her colleagues again reiterated how organised and capable the victim was. But none knew her intimately enough to have visited her flat or were able to give me a name of any of her closest friends or lovers. Some of her team are currently out of the country and may tell us more when they return."

Lawrence took over. "We interviewed the neighbours on both sides of Miss Carlisle's street. None of them had noticed anyone suspicious hanging around the property. But it's a busy thoroughfare and I would question if a stranger would really be clocked by residents."

Trudy added, "the fire escape for the building gives access to the roof. I spoke with the landlord and he says it was a requirement of the conversion, that the top flat had an escape route in a fire. But there's no evidence that one of the windows had been left open. I spoke again with the lady in the flat below, the one who found the victim. She says she didn't close a window when she was there."

Dani considered this. "Autumn had given her neighbour a key to her property. She'd only lived there a couple of months and hardly knew her. I wonder if she handed out keys to anyone else?"

"It's something you'd give to a best friend or

lover," Lawrence chipped in. "But we've no evidence that she had either."

Dani breathed in deeply. "I think we need to go back into Autumn's past. We need to visit the house she lived in before moving to Hillingdon and question her work colleagues at BA. She'd recently made a big change in her life. I'm sure the new job at Lomond offered her a better salary and prospects, but was there another reason why Autumn gave up her job and home?"

Lawrence nodded his agreement. "Gifford and Klein, can you check out Carlisle's previous employers? DC Singh, can you draft a press release? We want to appeal for witnesses who were on Camberwell Road at the time Carlisle was killed to come forward. There's a newsagents a couple of doors down, it would be worth asking in there too. People go in early for papers on a weekday."

The officers in the room dispersed to make a start on their tasks, leaving Dani and Nate Lawrence alone. The DI grinned. "Fancy a run down to the country, Dani, it is a lovely day?"

Dani was beginning to get to grips with the man's offbeat sense of humour. "Certainly, I'll just grab my coat."

*

It turned out to be one of those occasions when Dani missed having her simple, cropped hairstyle. DI Lawrence was driving the detectives to East Sussex in a silver Mercedes with its roof down, exposing them to a mild but ferocious breeze and some lovely views of the rolling countryside.

Dani had to shout above the engine noise. "This car can't possibly be police issue!"

Lawrence turned his head. "I've had it a good few years. I was a stockbroker in the City before I became a cop. I bought it then."

Dani nodded. This piece of information explained a great deal about the man. "Why the big career move!?" she yelled.

"The City is full of self-serving bastards. I'd made some cash, so it was time to take a job with value. I got on the fast-track at the Met and was a DC by the time I hit thirty."

Before Dani had a chance to reply, Lawrence abruptly swung the car to the left, exiting the main road and leading them along a winding lane with tall bushes flanking the vehicle on both sides.

The bushes suddenly fell away to reveal a charming settlement comprised of thatched cottages, a village green and a small stone church with a tall spire.

"This is it," Lawrence declared. "The village of Mitchling, East Sussex."

The cottage was easy enough to find, even though the Sat Nav had long since ceased to recognise the tiny lanes they were snaking through. It sat on the edge of the village and its name, *Maple Cottage*, was clearly displayed on a sign by the gate.

Dani climbed out of the car and stood at the low stone wall which enclosed its small, neat front garden. "What a beautiful house."

Lawrence came to stand beside her. "It's lovely. What the estate agents would call 'chocolate box'."

Dani frowned. "Why would Autumn move from such an idyllic location? The flat on Camberwell Road is nice enough inside, but that bloody plane noise. It was nightmarish."

Lawrence glanced about him at the surrounding countryside. "Trudy informed me that when Autumn was at BA, most of her flights were out of Gatwick.

She was within striking distance of the airport here. But with her move to Lomond, she needed to be nearer their base at Heathrow. A move was inevitable."

"Yes, I get that. But even so, the two properties make quite a contrast."

Whilst they were talking, a lady in her sixties had opened the door of the cottage and was approaching them along the path. "Can I help you?" She enquired in a forceful tone.

Lawrence got out his warrant card. "We're from the Metropolitan Police, madam. We wondered if you might answer a couple of question about the lady you bought this house from?"

Her brow creased, but she nodded her head and led the way inside.

Dani thought the interior was just as delightful as the outside. Mrs Forbes, retired headmistress, had filled the cottage with chintzy cushions and throws. A little black poodle was curled up in a Liberty patterned armchair.

"I've been here for three months now. I believe I have managed to make it my own. But the garden will be the real project for me." Mrs Forbes invited the detectives to take a seat in the low-ceilinged living room.

"It's a very nice property," Dani added politely.

Lawrence cleared his throat. "Did you meet the lady you bought the house from, Miss Autumn Carlisle?"

"Oh yes," Mrs Forbes replied. "She showed me around on one of my viewings. A refined young lady, I thought."

"I'm afraid she was found dead in her flat in Hillingdon several days ago."

The lady put her hand up to cover her mouth.

"My goodness! What awful news. She was so young and beautiful. The poor thing."

Dani shuffled forward in her seat. "Did Miss Carlisle give you an explanation as to why she was selling such a lovely cottage?"

"Well, she'd been offered a promotion, at another airline, she said. This meant moving closer to the city. I could tell she was sad to leave here, but I got the impression this was a new start for her."

Dani nodded. "Did you have any other contact with her, after you'd moved in? To forward mail, for example?"

"No, Miss Carlisle had instructed the post office to do that. I sensed she was an efficient person that way." Mrs Forbes clasped her hands in her lap. "I'm not one who likes to gossip."

"I'm sure, you aren't," Dani replied.

"But a few of the villagers here did talk about Miss Carlisle after I moved in. I suppose it's a sleepy sort of place without much news to speak of."

"What did these people say?" Lawrence inserted encouragingly.

"Well, they suggested that Miss Carlisle received a number of male visitors at the cottage."

"Could you give us the names of the villagers who told you this?" Lawrence got out his notebook expectantly.

"Oh, I don't want to get anyone into trouble. It was only tittle-tattle." The woman looked alarmed.

"We will be very discreet with our questioning, but it's imperative that we know the source of these rumours." Dani's expression became grave. "It is very likely that Miss Carlisle was murdered, you see."

"Goodness, then of course I must tell you, straight away."

Furnished with their list of names, Mrs Forbes led her visitors to the door.

"I hope you enjoy living here," Dani commented as they stepped out onto the path, the afternoon sun bathing the front garden in a golden glow.

"Oh, I shall, thank you. Although my first job will be to remove those tall maples round the back. They cut out all the natural light to the kitchen."

"They must be the reason the cottage got its name."

"Yes," the lady sounded wistful. "It's a shame to get rid of them for that very reason. But the trees are such an awful blight."

The detectives approached the car and open the doors to get in.

Mrs Forbes suddenly rushed forward to the gate, following them to the kerb. "I've just recalled something Miss Carlisle said, on my very first visit here."

"Go on," Dani was expectant.

"She said those trees were the main reason she chose to live here. The maples. She said they were the best thing about the house. It stuck in my mind, because to me, they were the very worst thing." She shrugged her shoulders bashfully. "I've no idea if that's important to you at all."

"I don't either," Dani replied earnestly. "But I'm extremely glad you told us."

Chapter 9

Lawrence pulled into the car park of a country pub which was positioned off the A22. The weather was pleasant enough for them to sit at one of the tables outside.

The DI sipped from a pint glass of coke. "Are you married, Dani? Any kids?"

Dani smiled. "My partner and I don't have children, no. How about you?"

He grimaced. "I worry that maybe I missed my chance with the whole marriage and family thing."

"Come off it, you're only young." Dani was once again amazed at the man's openness.

"Yeah, but when my mates were coupling up at college, I was fixated on making a million in the City. Then when I got the banking job, it absorbed all my time and energy. I had plenty of girlfriends, but none of those relationships stuck. Now I find myself in my mid-thirties and all the nice girls are taken."

"Maybe *nice* girls are over-rated. I didn't settle down until I was older than you. There are plenty of career women out there who are single." Dani took a gulp of her own drink.

"Well, I've yet to find one. I knew a girl once who really liked me. It freaked me out, so I didn't treat her very well. Now I think about her a lot."

"What is she doing now?" Dani knew that social media these days meant keeping tabs on the life choices of your exes was an easy enough task.

"Busy making house with her husband and two kids." He sighed. "I thought finding someone who you have a connection with and who cares for you in return was easy, so I threw it away when I had it."

Dani was starting to think Nate Lawrence's main problem was not the state of the singles' market, but his propensity towards self-pity. Either way, it was time to change the subject. "We have a description from the landlord of the King's Head in Mitchling. Autumn frequented the pub with the same man during the months before she moved out. There had been others, but this chap seemed like her latest and most regular companion."

"The couple who run the general store suggested Autumn had a new man at the cottage pretty much every month, although they couldn't provide much information about any of them. I got the sense they're both gossip merchants. One of the paper-round girls lives on the same road as Maple Cottage. She reported the comings and goings of male visitors there."

"I'm starting to understand why Autumn may have preferred the anonymity of the flat in London."

"Yet she didn't appear to have had a single visitor during her time on Camberwell Road, male or female."

Dani finished her drink. "Yes, it is odd. It's as if something changed for Autumn at that time, something more significant than a switch of jobs."

Lawrence glanced at his watch. "We'd better get back on the road. I'm holding a briefing at five."

Dani picked up her bag. "Sure, let's go. The traffic is only going to get worse if we hang around here."

*

Trudy Gifford perched on the edge of DI Lawrence's desk. Dani was seated beside her. The DC had returned from interviewing Autumn Carlisle's friends and colleagues at British Airways, where the woman had worked since graduating from college.

"It seems like Autumn had some good friends from her time at BA," Trudy began. "A couple of her colleagues went drinking with her in the evenings and stayed for weekends at her cottage."

"Did they mention the names of any boyfriends?" Dani asked.

"Yes, they gave me a couple of possible candidates that I still need to check out. It doesn't sound like Autumn had a lot of boyfriends, but she was at BA for over ten years, so there were a few men on the scene during that time."

"Had any of these friends seen Autumn in the last three months?" Lawrence interjected.

Trudy shook her head. "They said Autumn had lost touch since joining Lomond. It was put down to the hectic schedules of flight crew, no hard feelings were evident on either side."

Dani furrowed her brow. "But maybe an ex-boyfriend *had* taken offence at Autumn cutting him out of her life so abruptly. We need to check out the men on that list." She looked again at the description that had been given to her by the landlord of the King's Head in Mitchling. Autumn's regular companion was no taller than her, stocky in build, balding and aged around thirty-five. "I can't help feeling this description resembles Denny Lomond, CEO of Lomond Airlines. But he claims he and Autumn only became acquainted a few months ago. He gave the impression they had met up only in town."

Lawrence looked interested. "Maybe we should go back and talk to him again? Perhaps there was more to the relationship than he has let on?"

Dani nodded. "It's a good idea, but Lomond is a powerful man, if we return to question him again, I expect he'll get lawyered up in preparation."

"We'll have to take that chance. We've got precious few leads to chase up as it is."

Trudy got to her feet. "I'll start tracing the boyfriends, Boss."

Lawrence nodded his approval. "Dani and I will make that visit to the airport."

Chapter 10

Although the case was officially closed, DI Dermot Muir had continued to dig into the backgrounds of the German couple who died at the hotel. The newspaper speculation about the case had intrigued him.

Muir had learnt through his period of service with the diplomatic branch, that there were plenty of covert operations played out every day, all across the country, and that even the police had no knowledge of them.

DS Sharon Moffett brought him over a mug of coffee. She offered up an open bag of assorted pastries, which he politely declined. She pulled across one of the newspapers which was lying open on his desk. The piece on show was an analysis of the Berkley hotel deaths. "Are you still thinking about the Bauer case, Boss?"

He nodded. "It still feels like there are loose ends. Can a couple really die within hours of one another with no external factor intervening?"

Sharon dragged over a chair. "They were in their early seventies, both with serious heart problems. We have their doctor's testimony on that. The couple were in a foreign country and an unfamiliar bed. Sometimes, it doesn't take much for a person's system to close down."

"But *both* of them?" Dermot sipped his coffee, which was as good as it was possible to be from the machine in the department kitchen.

"I've heard of it happening. My great grandparents died within a few days of one another. They'd lived together for over sixty years, were barely apart in the last twenty of their lives. Couples can become physically and emotionally interdependent. It's nothing sinister, just our hormones and stuff getting in sync." Sharon reached for a Danish pastry from the bag and bit into it, sending a snowfall of icing sugar down the front of her blouse.

Muir did his best not to look at the resultant spillage. "But there must have been a *trigger.*"

Sharon considered this. In the case of her great-grandparents it was the news of her uncle's death in a motorcycle accident which had precipitated their demise. The family hypothesis was the old pair didn't want to carry on after that, the grief was too much. "Perhaps they'd received a piece of bad news. We could always contact the son and daughter again and ask them?"

Muir shook his head. "We reassured Stefan Bauer the case would be passed onto the Fiscal's office where a verdict of death by natural causes was the most likely outcome. If I contact them again, it will only shake things up."

Sharon stood. "That's true enough, and we need to get the reports written up for when DCI Bevan returns from London."

"Aye, you're right." Muir shuffled the newspapers into a pile and shoved them in his drawer. "My girlfriend would be fuming if she thought I was making extra work for myself."

"While the DCI is away, we can control our own workload. Don't make life more difficult for yourself than it needs to be, Boss."

Muir watched his colleague return to her desk, where DS Calder made a grab for the bag of pastries. He smiled to himself. But that niggling, persistent sense of doubt still remained, no matter how hard he tried to push it down.

*

Trudy Gifford was led through a carpeted hallway with leather sofas flanking the walls at strategic points. The woman guiding her stopped outside one of the doors. She gave a light knock before opening it and nodding for the DC to enter.

The office was as softly furnished as the rest of the building. Trudy approached the desk, flattening the thick pile of the carpet with her sturdy shoes. "Mr Colbert? I'm DC Gifford from Hammersmith CID. Thank you for agreeing to speak with me."

The man stood, putting out his hand. "Please, call me Noel. Take a seat, detective. You wanted to ask me about Autumn Carlisle?"

"That's correct, sir. One of her co-workers at BA suggested you two had been an item a couple of years back?"

He nodded, running his fingers through his sandy hair. "I didn't know she was dead until you called. It was one hell of a shock."

"When did you break up?"

"It was the summer of 2016. We went on holiday to Florida but argued a lot. After we got back, we agreed to cool things off. By the Christmas we weren't in contact at all."

"How did you meet her?"

"I'm a regular flyer with BA. I got to know Autumn when she worked in Business Class. I asked her out after a business trip I took to Frankfurt. When we returned, we went for drinks near the offices here and were together for the next eighteen months."

"Did you visit her cottage in Mitchling?"

"Yeah, I was there a lot. The cottage is much more pleasant than my flat."

"Did you know Autumn moved out of the cottage three months ago?"

Noel crinkled his forehead. "No, I hadn't heard that. As I said, we weren't in touch any more. But I find that surprising. She loved the cottage. We spoke about me moving in someday, there may even have been mention of kids frolicking in the lovely garden. That place was home to her."

"Her job move to Lomond Airlines meant she needed to be closer to Heathrow. It makes sense for that reason."

Noel looked genuinely taken aback. "Had Autumn taken a job at Lomond? Bloody Hell! Things definitely *had* changed."

"How so?" Trudy was intrigued.

"Autumn was always complaining about Lomond opening up routes to international destinations and undercutting BA on prices. She said it would be passenger comfort, service and safety that would ultimately be compromised. She hardly shut-up about it, to be honest."

"Perhaps Denny Lomond made her an offer she couldn't refuse?"

"He must have done." The man looked dazed. "I suppose it's no more incredible than the idea of Autumn taking her own life."

"You don't think she would have committed suicide?"

He shrugged. "The woman I knew was full of life. She loved travel, had good friends around the world. When I asked her to give up the job and settle down with me, she wouldn't have it. That's why we split. Her life was too enjoyable to give up for a relationship, so why the hell would she end it?"

Trudy nodded her head. Why indeed. "We now have reason to think the cause of death wasn't necessarily suicide. Did you meet many of Autumn's friends? An ex-boyfriend before you perhaps?"

"I don't think Autumn had many serious relationships before me. But I met her mates in Amsterdam, I got the impression they were her closest. We stayed for a weekend in the February of 2015, it was fun."

"Autumn crewed a flight to Amsterdam in the week before her death," Trudy commented.

Noel leaned forward. "She would undoubtedly have hooked up with Lucas and Sofie. Autumn never missed a chance to see them."

Trudy asked eagerly, "do you have any contact details for them?"

He considered this. "Actually, I still have Lucas's number on my phone. I added it whilst we were over there, so we could meet up for dinner and stuff. It's three years old, mind you."

"That doesn't matter. I'd like to have it, if I may."

Noel dug in his pocket for a black, glossy smartphone. "Of course you can have it. Perhaps Lucas and Sofie will have a better idea of what the heck had been going on with Autumn recently. Because her behaviour certainly doesn't sound like the lady *I* knew."

Trudy jotted down the number gratefully.

Noel slumped back into his plush, leather chair, the information he'd been given only just seeming to have sunk in. "Do you think Autumn might have been *murdered?*"

Trudy nodded. "It's a possibility we're looking into, Sir."

He shook his head sadly. "Why did she leave that sleepy little village to come to this heartless old city?" He glanced out of the window as if to highlight his words. "It wasn't as if Autumn was naïve about how evil the world could be."

Trudy frowned deeply. "What do you mean by

that, Mr Colbert?"

He peered down his angular nose at the detective. "Well, I happen to know that early in her career she had a nasty encounter with one of her passengers. It was following a flight to one of the Egyptian resorts. This chap had noticed Autumn on the plane and then followed her after they landed. I think there was some type of physical attack. She reported it to the police. He got a caution and a ban from BA flights. It wasn't a huge deal, but it made Autumn circumspect, you know?"

Trudy had rapidly noted down the details as the man spoke. "Do you know when this happened exactly?"

"Oh, it was before the two of us met, a good decade back I'd say. But there must be records of it somewhere, if she went to the police?"

"Yes," Trudy agreed. "There certainly would." She stood to leave. "Thank you for your assistance, Mr Colbert. You've given me plenty to follow up."

Chapter 11

This time DCI Dani Bevan visited the headquarters of Lomond Airlines, the CEO wasn't on hand to greet her. She and Nate waited in a long, dark corridor for Denny Lomond's PA to finally make an appearance.

"I will accompany you to one of our boardrooms, Detectives. Unfortunately, Mr Lomond is out of the building on business. But I believe you wished to speak with a member of our staff by the name of Kathy Brice? She is being fetched for you." The woman delivered her words over one shoulder, as she strode along the corridor, pausing halfway down to swing open a door for them.

Dani entered first, into a room filled with a glass table and leather chairs, bordered by a series of windows looking out over one of the flight terminals. "We really do need to speak with Mr Lomond himself," she added with emphasis.

"Yes, and I will make an appointment for you. But today isn't good for him, I'm afraid. He's in high-level discussions with the pilots' union, there's talk of a possible strike." She wrinkled her heavily-made up face to illustrate the seriousness of the situation.

Nate sighed heavily. "At the present time, we are asking Mr Lomond to voluntarily aid us with our enquiries, but if he refuses to see us, we will have to have our conversation at Hammersmith Police station."

The PA backed out of the room. "I'll pass that on to him, Detective Inspector. In the meantime, I'll order a pot of coffee for you and Ms Brice."

When she had left, Dani lifted her eyebrows. "I don't reckon we'll get hold of Denny Lomond any time soon, certainly not without his corporate lawyers in tow. It sounds like he's in the midst of some kind of industrial dispute."

"He should try paying his staff properly, that might resolve the problem," Nate muttered darkly.

"Then we wouldn't get our cheap package holidays to the Continent," Dani added playfully.

"I wouldn't fly with Lomond Airlines anyway," he glanced out of one of the vast windows at the huge aeroplanes taxiing towards the runway. "You wonder what safety checks get overlooked in order to operate on such low fares. It's not bloody worth it."

The door re-opened and a plump woman pushed a tray holding a coffee pot and a set of cups to the end of the conference table. Hot on her heels entered a woman in her twenties, dressed in the Lomond Airlines cabin uniform. She smiled broadly at the detectives, as the canteen assistant slipped out behind her.

"You must be Kathy Brice?" Dani enquired, indicating the woman should take a seat.

"That's right. My supervisor said you wanted to get hold of me? I've been in Florida for the last couple of days. I needed to wait until my scheduled flight back."

"That's okay," Dani continued. "Did your supervisor tell you we wanted to talk to you about Autumn Carlisle?"

A shadow passed across Kathy's painted features. "Yes, he said. But I already gave a statement to the lady detective last week?"

Nate leant forward. "Since then, new information has come to light. We believe Ms Carlisle may have been murdered. This means we need to speak to everyone again."

Her mouth dropped open, revealing two rows of perfectly white, neat teeth. "*Christ.* That's awful. I know her being found dead was bad, but to be murdered in your own bedroom." She visibly shuddered.

Dani addressed her in a level tone. "DC Gifford got the impression you didn't like Autumn Carlisle very much. She said you weren't impressed with her as a cabin supervisor?"

She crossed her arms over her chest defensively. "I had nothing against her personally. It's just the management kept raving about how brilliant she was with the passengers and such. Except, I didn't think she was so great." Kathy leant forward conspiratorially. "On that last trip to Amsterdam, Miss Carlisle looked a mess. She was sweating heaps and her hands were shaking when she poured the drinks. I thought she was either badly hungover or had the flu. I nearly said something."

"You are the only witness we've interviewed who has contradicted the assertion Miss Carlisle was extremely good at her job." Nate narrowed his eyes as he casually assessed the woman seated before them.

Kathy shrugged. "Like I said, the management loved her. Particularly Mr Lomond." A flicker of a smirk lifted the corners of her red lips.

Dani seized on the implication. "Are you suggesting there was something more to their relationship than the purely professional?"

"I couldn't say for sure. But I watched them together in meetings, they seemed pretty friendly. I mean, I know they were both Scottish, but there was a closeness between them that went deeper than that, I could tell."

Nate frowned. "How long have you worked for Lomond Airlines, Ms Brice?"

"Four years this October. I completed my travel and tourism degree at the uni in Bristol, got the job straight after."

"And when the supervisor position came up at Lomond, did you apply?"

The woman's defensive posture returned, she seemed to almost be hugging herself. "As a matter of fact, I did. I'm a graduate and I'd worked for Lomond for years. It didn't make sense to me that Miss Carlisle was brought in from outside."

"So, you had reason to feel resentful towards her, to feel the supervisory role should have been yours?"

Kathy seemed to suddenly realise the implication of her words. "No! I didn't like her much; she was distant towards me and the other crew, we certainly knew she was the boss. But I'm not making any of this up! She was a basket case on that flight to Amsterdam, I swear it!"

Nate put up a hand to calm the situation down. "Okay, fine. We get the point. But I'm going to need to ask you about your movements on the night of the 3rd July and the early morning of the 4th. I'll require as much detail as you can provide, please."

The woman fell silent, wiping her tongue across her lips as if they had suddenly become dry. "Yeah, no problem. I was at my boyfriend's place, I think. I'll just need to check my diary."

Dani stood. "That's okay, as long as you email the information to DI Lawrence by the end of the day."

The detectives left her looking shell-shocked, sitting very still in her chair. They emerged into the dingy corridor.

"You don't really think she's a suspect, do you?" Dani asked incredulously.

"No," Nate replied. "I just really disliked her. Thought it might do her good to stew for a bit."

Dani chuckled. "Yes, I didn't warm to her either. But I still believe she was telling us the truth about Autumn."

"Yeah, she annoyed the hell out of me, but I never said I didn't believe her."

*

The only hotel rooms available in the vicinity of the Hammersmith Police Station were in no-frills establishments designed for the use of passengers utilising the airport. This suited Dani well. The DCS was happy for her to liaise with the Met over the Carlisle case, particularly now it was looking like murder. But he'd not gone as far as to grant her a budget. She could always put in a claim with Lawrence and his team to cover her bill, but as it was her who shook things up in the first place, she felt reluctant to do so.

The room was clean and functional. There was even an armchair where she could sit and review her notes. The only distraction was the noise of the aircraft landing at nearby Heathrow which was discernible even through the thickly glazed hotel windows. Dani assumed you got used to it. But for tonight, she was prepared to use the spongy earplugs that were supplied with the free toiletries.

The file Trudy had given Dani was thin. Autumn appeared not to have kept many personal effects at her flat. She made a mental note to check with Mike and Betsy as to whether their daughter stored any items at their place after moving from the cottage in Sussex. The remainder of the woman's belongings must have ended up somewhere.

A leather-bound diary slipped out onto Dani's lap. A brief flick through the pages indicated Autumn used it to keep track of her schedule at the airport. There was also a list of names and addresses at the back. Dani noted the reference to the couple in Amsterdam mentioned by Noel Colbert. Trudy was planning to speak with them once the Dutch police gave her the green light.

The list seemed depressingly short; maybe forty people in total, of which a decent proportion looked like relatives living around the north east of Scotland. Dani assumed it was difficult to make connections when you spent most of your life in transit to other countries.

The detective sighed; every single one of these names would have to be checked and alibis gained for the night of Autumn's murder. But Dani felt sure the woman's murderer was not listed within these pages. If the killer was someone she knew, then it was a person Autumn would not have given respectability to by listing them in her address book. Dani's experience told her that the sparsity of Autumn's possessions indicated a person who kept secrets. There was no surface clutter in this woman's life, which didn't mean there wasn't an almighty mess lurking beneath that surface.

Dani placed the diary back into its folder. She levered herself off the chair. It was still early, but she resolved to get a decent night's sleep before the debriefing with DI Lawrence in the morning.

Chapter 12

When Dani finally awoke, in a groggy haze, twisted amongst the polyester sheets of the overheated hotel room, she automatically fumbled for her mobile phone. The screen notified her of a dozen missed calls. All from DI Lawrence.

"*Shit*," she rasped, whilst dragging out the complimentary foam earplugs and hurling them across the bed. "*Bloody things!*" The phone buzzed again, this time she immediately accepted the call. "DCI Bevan."

"Bevan, thank God you've picked up, I was starting to get worried about you." Nate Lawrence's tone was more curious than genuinely concerned.

"Sorry, I must have slept heavily and missed your calls. What's the problem?"

"I'm at Heathrow, Terminal 1. You'd better come down and see for yourself. I'll send a patrol car over to the hotel to pick you up."

"I'll be ready in ten minutes."

*

The airport terminal was busy. Queues snaked in and out of the barriers herding passengers to the baggage desks. The concourse was packed with trolleys and people standing, staring up at the myriad of screens suspended from the ceilings, as if in a trance.

When she finally arrived, Dani saw DI Lawrence amongst a group of airport police and security guards. Denny Lomond was discernible within the throng. It must be serious, she thought.

Nate stepped out of the group to intercept her. "I

didn't get an email back from Kathy Brice last night, so I called her home number. Her boyfriend said he was worried about her, as she'd not returned from work yet."

"She was usually prompt home, then?"

"Yep, it would seem so. They share a flat in Kilburn. When she was in the country, Kathy got the tube straight there after her shift finished."

Dani glanced at the throng of officials and felt a mounting sense of dread. "What did you do next?"

"I called Lomond Airlines to see if she was still there. Lomond's PA, Diane Martin, the evasive one, did a sweep of the offices but couldn't find her, she had stayed late to type up the minutes from Lomond's meeting with the pilots' union. It seems they've only got a few days to avert strike action. That's when the airport security alarm went off and the place was evacuated. I realised then something was wrong, so I headed straight down here, that was around 10pm. I tried to call you to see if you wanted to tag along?"

Dani cleared her throat. "Sorry about that."

"Not a problem. The airport was swarming with cops by the time I got here anyway. One of the cleaners found a body in the toilet cubicle near one of the departure lounges. They've closed off gate 52 and diverted flights to another gate for the time being. The anti-terrorist guys have assessed the situation. They decided there was no need to shut the entire airport."

Dani felt the blood run icy in her veins. "Was it Kathy?"

Nate nodded solemnly. "She'd been strangled, possibly with a thin strap – a belt perhaps. The pathologist reckoned she died between 6pm and 9pm. Because it was beyond passport control, the ladies' toilet she was found in tended to be quiet."

"But still, this is a busy airport. The killer was taking one hell of a risk." Dani shook her head in disbelief. "What was Kathy doing at the terminal gate at that time of day? Why wasn't she in the Lomond Airlines offices?"

"We'll know more when we can question all the staff. But Mr Lomond says it was a gate Kathy Brice often worked from. Perhaps she was picking up a personal item from the departure desk?"

Dani wrinkled her brow. "Or meeting someone?"

"Well, you'd need to be a staff member or have a boarding pass to be allowed in that area."

Dani nodded. "We'll require a list of all the passengers flying out through that gate yesterday afternoon."

"Sure. I've got a couple of DCs questioning the staff at Lomond's offices. We need to find the last person who saw her alive. It will help us to narrow down the time of death."

"Let's hope it wasn't us," Dani said with a grimace.

Nate sighed heavily. "We left before lunch, so I imagine not. But I do wonder if this happened because we talked to her yesterday."

Dani didn't reply. It was difficult to draw any other conclusion. "Is she still *in situ*?"

Nate shook his head. "The pathologist removed the body last night. But I'll take you to view the scene."

*

The corridor was empty, except for the security guards manning the gate. Nate flashed his warrant card and led Dani towards the police tape and plastic barriers cordoning off the entrance to the toilets. The SOCOs were still milling in and out.

"Can we go in?" Nate asked one of the techs who was holding a clip-board.

He pointed to a pile of pale blue shoe covers. "If you put those on and stick to the trays, sure. We're nearly finished now, anyway."

Dani surveyed the scene. The room had only four cubicles in it. From the positioning of the SOCO trays, the body of Kathy Brice had been found in the one furthest from the door. She stepped gingerly towards the entrance to the cubicle. Nate was at her shoulder.

"The door wasn't locked, but the cleaner was having trouble opening it fully. She thought maybe someone had collapsed in there, so she gave it a shove." Nate dipped his head. "The body was slumped on the toilet seat with the legs splayed out. A narrow, reddish bruise was evident around the neck. Scuffs to the walls indicate a minor scuffle, but it seems Kathy was quickly subdued. There was no other kind of assault; her clothes weren't disturbed that we could identify. The *PM* will tell us more."

"Do we think this was a male attacker?"

Nate shrugged. "Kathy had a slight build. I reckon a strong woman could have done it."

Dani agreed. These days, the physical differences between men and women were negligible. A woman who regularly visited the gym would be perfectly capable of taking on a man of similar size and build. "And the killer used a garotte of some kind. That would reduce the amount of brute strength required to throttle her."

Dani took a step outside the cubicle and glanced towards the window above the sinks. "Where does that lead?"

"I'm not sure, but I'll check it out."

"There must be CCTV all over this airport. Any

covering the toilet door?"

Nate frowned to indicate the news wasn't good. "I've already asked the airport guys. There's a couple of cameras at the departure gate and a few at passport control, but none on this corridor."

"Damn it. Do you think the killer knew that?"

"It's possible."

"But they will still be on camera somewhere at the airport. This place must have the tightest security in the country."

"You'd have certainly thought so," Nate added, with just the tiniest hint of irony to his tone.

Chapter 13

Betsy Carlisle tugged at the lead of the small white dog that was pulling her dangerously close to the edge of the towpath. The still waters of the Forth and Clyde Canal lay a few feet below.

"Come to heel, Dodie!" Betsy called in frustration. She turned to their companion. "I apologise for her behaviour, Rhodri. She's still only a wee pup."

"God knows why we made the decision to get her," Mike muttered irritably. "These small dogs are a bugger to train."

Betsy turned to her husband. "Dodie has been a great comfort to me since Autumn's passing and she has to *you*, too, if you're honest."

The man grumbled under his breath but didn't openly disagree.

"We had a lovely Lab when the boys were young. Once they've grown up a bit and calmed down, a dog can be a wonderful companion." Rhodri bent over to pat the puppy on its fluffy head.

Betsy nodded. "We've had dogs for all the years we've been in Cumbernauld. Old Lilly died last year. Dodie is from the same breeder. We bought her before we got the dreadful news from London. I wonder now if we would have done so if we knew what was going to happen."

The woman's words hung in the warm afternoon air alongside the tiny flies that hovered just above the waterline.

There seemed to be no answer to this particular question. It was clear that Betsy didn't expect one. Rhodri took the opportunity to steer the couple towards a bench by the side of the canal bank.

"I've got some information for you, from DCI Bevan."

Betsy lifted the pup into her lap and clutched it tightly. The animal buried its head inside her jacket. "What is it?"

"The footprint found in your daughter's bedroom meant that DI Lawrence was able to re-open his investigations. They were interviewing Autumn's friends and colleagues once more."

"That's *good* news," Mike responded firmly.

"Yes, but one of the girls they spoke to again was found dead yesterday evening. She'd been strangled."

Betsy squeezed the dog so hard it let out a tiny yelp. "Sweet Jesus in Heaven. What does this mean?"

Rhodri rested his hand on her arm. "Danielle doesn't know just yet. The girl who was killed – a woman, really, was called Kathy. She was a bit younger than your daughter. She was in Autumn's team at Lomond Airlines. She'd been more candid with the detectives in her interviews than the other witnesses."

Mike's body jerked to attention. "I think I recall Autumn talking about this woman. Was she a member of the cabin crew?"

Rhodri nodded. "That's right."

"Autumn complained about her when she stayed with us. She said there was a member of her team who was being awkward about taking orders from her. She suspected this Kathy girl had gone for the supervisor job herself, so there was an element of sour grapes. Autumn was thinking about giving her a formal warning. She said her behaviour was insubordinate."

"Hmm," Rhodri rubbed his snow-white beard. "I'll pass that information onto Danielle."

"Why would anyone want to *kill* her?" Betsy's voice was shrill. "Was it the same person who killed Autumn?"

Mike got to his feet and indicated that Rhodri should follow him. They took a few steps away from the bench and stood by the bank of the waterway. A flock of geese had just landed on its surface, disturbing the calm and causing the canal boats to rock gently in their moorings. "I don't think we should talk about this in front of Betsy. It's best we get her home now."

"Of course. I'm terribly sorry if I upset her. I just thought you would both want to know the latest developments."

"Yes, yes, we do. But Betsy hasn't always been well. She has a delicate nervous disposition. The death of Autumn had been bad enough, but at least she's just about coping. I'm simply not sure how much more stress she can take."

"I didn't realise this." Rhodri's expression was solemn. "Is Betsy on a regime of care with her local health authority? I can suggest some very good practitioners in your area. She could even come to Glasgow for treatment."

Mike rubbed his hands down his fleece irritably. "We've done it all, over the years. She takes some meds now which keep things on an even keel. But her problems are deeper rooted than the average. There's not much can be done for her."

Rhodri wasn't convinced this would be the case. He knew that all psychological illnesses could be treated with a reasonable amount of success. In his long experience, *all* sufferers felt their case was more acute than any one else's. It didn't mean they couldn't be cured. But the professor said nothing, sensing Mike was keen to end the discussion. "Then let's make our way back to the house. I promise I'll say no more on the subject."

*

The Carlisles' property was a stone built semi-detached house on the outskirts of the town. The rumble of the M80 motorway was far enough away to be just a distant hum on the breeze.

Betsy had made a pot of coffee which stood on a table in the conservatory. Rhodri stood to sip from his cup, gazing out into the well-tended garden, where Dodie was frolicking in the late afternoon sunshine with a ball. The professor had known Mike for about fifteen years. For the entirety of that time they had lived in this house.

As if she could tell what her guest was thinking, Betsy suddenly said, "Autumn was ten years old when we moved here. She attended the high school in town."

Rhodri turned his head. "Where were you before that?"

Betsy busied herself adding milk and sugar to her cup. "Oh, we were in the Highlands for a while. That's where Autumn was born. Before that, I spent some time abroad."

Rhodri put down his cup and saucer. "I didn't know that. Whereabouts in the Highlands were you?"

Betsy was about to answer when a ferocious barking ensued from the direction of the garden. Mike came rushing out of the sitting room. He bolted through the open doors of the conservatory, chasing after his recalcitrant pet, attempting to grab the dog by its collar.

"Oh dear." Betsy was on her feet too. "Dodie must have caught sight of next-door's rabbit. The little girl has a habit of letting it hop about on the lawn. We live in dread of Dodie getting through the fence and attacking it."

Mike had finally managed to clip the lead onto the boisterous puppy. "We'd better keep her inside for a bit," he instructed his wife in a stern tone.

Rhodri pulled the French doors closed behind his friend. "And I'd better make a move back to the city. The traffic will be awful if I leave it much later."

"Of course," Betsy gushed. "I'll go and find your coat."

Chapter 14

It took only half an hour to drive out to Denny Lomond's riverside property in Henley-on-Thames, but to Dani it felt like a million miles away from the urban sprawl of Hammersmith.

Nate had to jump out of the driving seat of his Mercedes to explain the purpose of his visit through the grill of Lomond's security system. Eventually, the tall iron gates barring their progress began to slowly slide apart.

Dani took in her surroundings. The house was modern in design, but the garden was traditionally landscaped. The lush green lawn ended at the waterside. A small wooden jetty projected out into the river. A smart motor cruiser was moored to one of its posts. "Nice place," she called to her companion. "I bet there's no aircraft noise here."

"I imagine he was very careful to ensure there wasn't." Nate parked on the gravel drive in front of a block of garages. Beyond one of the doors, he could see the headlights of a classic Ferrari, the type of model he'd have given anything himself to own.

Denny Lomond was crunching across the limestone chips to greet them. The man was out of his work suit and wearing a designer polo shirt with a pair of fawn chinos. "DI Lawrence, DCI Bevan! I'm glad we've finally had a chance to catch up. I just wish it was under better circumstances."

The detectives followed him into the house. The décor was immaculate. A bowl on a dresser by the front door held a fresh bouquet of flowers. Despite the neatness, Dani wasn't picking up on any signs this was a family home. The walls were lined with what appeared to be original pieces of modern art, but no photographs of people. It reminded her oddly of Autumn's flat in Hillingdon, which was similarly devoid of the common indicators of family life.

Denny stopped when they reached the large kitchen. Patio doors were open onto the garden. "Would you like coffee? It's freshly brewed?"

"Yes, thank you," Dani added.

Nate leant his lanky form against the central island, impatient to begin their questioning. "I visited Kathy Brice's parents in Surrey this morning. They are devastated."

Denny turned to face the DI. "I'm going to see them myself over the next few days. It is a very sad time for Lomond Airlines. To lose two of our staff in such a short period. It's heart-breaking. We are a small company; a family in many respects."

Dani interjected, "we've spoken with your employees. We know that Kathy was last seen at her desk around 5.30pm. We suspect she left the offices and made her way down to departure gate 52 not long after this. Where were you during this time, Mr Lomond?"

The man poured coffee into three cups. He lifted his dark eyes so they made contact with Dani's. "I was in a highly charged meeting with the head of the pilots' union and a bunch of both our lawyers. The meeting started at 3.30pm and dragged on until 8. You can ask Diane to confirm. The poor woman had to stay late to type up the minutes. I needed to draft a letter setting out our agreement by first thing the following morning, otherwise all our flights would have been grounded."

"And you were in the meeting room for that entire time?" Nate reached for his cup of coffee and practically downed it in one gulp.

Denny let out a humourless laugh. "I probably

needed to answer the call of nature at least once. But I don't expect I was gone long enough to find my way to gate 52 and strangle poor Kathy to death."

Dani decided to change tack. "When we spoke a few days ago, you said you'd only met Autumn Carlisle on a handful of occasions before she came to work for you. We have a sworn statement from a witness who described a frequent companion of Autumn's in her old village of Mitchling. This man was seen regularly in the local pub with her. The description sounded a lot like you, Mr Lomond."

Denny creased his brow. "Well, I promise you, detective, it wasn't. I met Autumn for lunch twice and that was all. I can probably dig out the receipts for both occasions from my accounts. I classed them as business meetings and therefore they are in my expenses folder." His sipped from his cup. "Our relationship was purely professional."

Nate leant forward. "Kathy Brice suggested you and Autumn were on very friendly terms. She implied there was a sexual relationship between you. Within a few hours of making this suggestion, she was dead."

Denny shrugged. "I don't wish to speak ill of the dead, but Kathy was prone to spread rumours about her colleagues. I received several written complaints about her conduct. In fact, her last supervisor had her on a formal warning. There was no sexual relationship between myself and Autumn Carlisle. I would suggest that if Kathy was spreading untruths about this, she could very well have been telling lies about other people, too. There may have been any number of individuals who had reason to dislike Ms Brice."

Dani had already considered this possibility. She suspected Kathy had made herself an assortment of enemies. Which made their job even harder.

Nate had opened his mouth to say something more when a tall figure appeared at the doors to the garden. Both detectives turned in the direction of the new arrival. His features were in shadow, but his outline was imposing and broad, cutting out much of the natural light to the room.

"I've cleared most of the weeds from the bank, Denny. It should be easier to get the boat out now." The man stepped into the kitchen, eyeing the visitors carefully. His accent was unmistakeably Scots.

"Thank you." Denny turned to the detectives. "This is my younger brother, John. He's been living here for the past couple of years."

The taller man nodded in recognition. "I'll get back to work, Den. I want to give the boat a wash down while there's still enough light."

"Sure John, but make certain you come in for dinner."

The man exited as swiftly as he had arrived.

Denny sighed. "My brother has rather taken on the role of groundsman here. I've told him umpteen times he doesn't need to. I think he enjoys it."

"Is it just you and your brother living here?" Dani glanced around the pristine kitchen, which appeared little used.

"My wife died three years ago from cancer. We'd not got around to starting a family by the time she was diagnosed and then it was too late."

"I'm very sorry." Dani put down her cup.

"When Kelly passed away, I decided to open up the offices down here in London, operate the airline out of Heathrow. She'd never wanted to leave Scotland, and with her gone, I didnae much want to stay. John needed somewhere to go when his marriage broke up. He came here. We keep one another company, so he's never left."

Dani nodded. She now understood the unusual

atmosphere in the house. It was a sanctuary for two bachelors, both with a melancholy past.

Nate got to his feet. "Thank you for your time, Mr Lomond. If we could have those receipts from your lunch meetings with Ms Carlisle, I'd appreciate it."

Denny put out his hand. "Certainly, detective. I'll email them over to your department as soon as possible." He glanced out of the patio doors at the fading sunlight. "Do you mind seeing yourselves out? I want to give John a hand with the boat."

"Of course." Dani led the way to the front door. When they were both seated in the car she said, "what did you make of that? Do you think he was telling the truth about his relationship with Autumn?"

Nate manoeuvred carefully down the gravel driveway before answering. "I got the feeling he wasn't in a sexual relationship with Autumn, but that doesn't mean they didn't have a stronger association than he is making out."

"I can't help considering Denny's point about Kathy Brice being a vicious gossip. Perhaps her rumour spreading made a dangerous enemy of someone else at Lomond Airlines?"

"Yeah, I need to feed that back to the team. Maybe another of Ms Brice's colleagues decided it was time to shut her up. Denny claimed their organisation was like a 'family', yet he's facing a walk-out from his pilots and two of his staff have just been murdered. I don't buy it."

As they exited through the gateway, Dani twisted back to take another look at the house and garden. The figure of John Lomond was silhouetted against the evening light. He was standing by the jetty watching them leave. His unfaltering gaze made Dani involuntarily shudder.

Chapter 15

Dermot Muir felt a prickle of uncertainty run down his spine as he stood to address the assembled detectives. He could pick out DS Calder's scowling face within the crowd, it made him momentarily hesitate before he finally spoke. "As you are all aware, DCI Bevan is currently liaising with the Met on a murder case down in London. There's been another death and the DCI will be involved in the investigation for the foreseeable future."

Several muted groans were audible within the group. A sea of hostile faces were directed his way.

Muir squared his shoulders and took a breath. "The DCS has asked me to take charge of the section until DCI Bevan returns." He paused. The barrage of abuse he was half anticipating didn't come.

Calder's hand shot up. "Does this mean you're gettin' the office, Guv?" This comment was met with a few chuckles.

Muir decided that if this was the worst he was going to get; new on the job, a maternity cover and suddenly the boss, he'd lucked out. "That's right, Andy. And you'll be my new tea-boy." This comment received even more laughs, so the DI decided to quit whilst he was ahead.

As the detectives made their way back to their desks, Muir caught up with Sharon. "The team took that better than I was expecting."

Sharon smiled. "We all knew the DCI was tied up in this London thing. Most of the DCs were terrified that DCS Douglas was going to take over the division himself." She patted him on the shoulder. "You're definitely the lesser of two evils."

Muir wasn't quite sure what to say to this, so he returned to his temporary office without uttering another word.

*

Muir allowed his eyes to run over the gentle contours of DCI Bevan's desk. It had been left reasonably tidy, but her in-tray remained half-full and there were scatterings of stationery and personal effects piled at the edges of the polished oak surface.

The DI had no intention of making a play for Bevan's position. The DCS had made it perfectly clear this was a temporary promotion, but that his performance would be recognised in future appraisals. He just needed to keep things ticking over, act like a caretaker until the real boss returned. The sub-text of the conversation was that Muir shouldn't stir up any trouble in Bevan's absence.

But Muir was still pre-occupied by the death of the couple at the Berkley Hotel. The idea of closing the book on it didn't sit well with him. He had a contact at Interpol from his days at the diplomatic branch. On his own initiative, he'd requested any files they possessed in relation to Klaus Bauer.

In life, Mr Bauer was a respected retired scientist living on the outskirts of Frankfurt. Before he retired, Bauer had worked for an international pharmaceutical company based in the city. He'd been a research chemist who worked on several medicines over the years that had received patents. His career was celebrated by the company in a retirement party in 2010.

Muir glanced at the notes his Interpol source had

added to the file. Klaus Bauer was a respected German citizen with no criminal convictions or cautions. The only reason Interpol had information pertaining to him was because of his work for the government during the Soviet occupation of East Germany up to 1990.

Klaus Bauer was born in the early 1940s. Under the rule of the GDR he attended one of the polytechnic secondary schools in the suburb of East Berlin where he grew up. His parents both worked in factories and his schooling lasted six days a week. The regime was strict, but Klaus excelled at science.

Entry to university in the GDR was extremely limited. Klaus would have been one of the top two or three performing students in his cohort. According to Interpol, he obtained his place at the University of Leipzig through an industrial apprenticeship. Once Klaus had graduated, the information about his life became sparse. There was a record of his marriage to Greta in 1971. They were living in Berlin during this time. There were also the registers of the births of their two children, both born in the mid-seventies, but no more about his professional life.

The file concluded Klaus Bauer would have most likely worked for the East German government upon graduation. His skills as a biochemist may have been used in the production of medicines, but also in the development of weapons. No records of his work during those years survived the collapse of the GDR in 1990.

Klaus and Greta Bauer left Berlin with their two young children in 1991 when Klaus got a job at the pharma company in Frankfurt. The family had remained there ever since; apparently law-abiding citizens well-regarded by colleagues and neighbours.

Muir lifted his head with a start when there was a knock at the door. He automatically closed the file.

Sharon was peering at him through the plexiglass panel. He gestured for her to enter.

"We're going for a drink later, Boss? Thought you may want to join us?"

Muir glanced down at the thin file, which he had finished reading in less than thirty minutes. "Sure, why not. I can't stay long, though." He thought of his girlfriend waiting back at their flat. However busy her day seemed to have been, she always made it home before him.

"That's what they all say!" Sharon offered with a laugh, closing the door behind her and leaving Muir to his own thoughts.

Chapter 16

The streets around Kilburn High Road were stationary with traffic. Nate abruptly swung his car into a narrow space at the kerbside of a residential street.

"We'll have to walk from here," he announced.

Dani examined the housing that predominated in this part of north-west London as they navigated the A-Z to reach the address they wanted. An assortment of modern and art deco blocks of flats sat alongside terraces of dark red stone. Some of the houses had been renovated, but others appeared tatty and uncared for. The DCI noted the absence of the low flying aircraft traffic which plagued the area where Autumn had lived. This made the postcode vastly more desirable, in her opinion.

The block of flats they were looking for was one of the more modern variety. The entrance hall housed a carpeted stairwell which was wide and bright. Nate reached the third floor ahead of Dani. He pressed the bell beneath a label which denoted the occupants.

Tom Birch open the door with an attitude of resignation. His head of floppy, chestnut hair was hung low.

"Mr Birch? I'm DI Lawrence from the Metropolitan Police. We spoke earlier today. This is my colleague, DCI Bevan. May we come inside?"

He mumbled a reply and wandered into the flat, stopping when he reached a bright living room, where a studio shot of Tom and Kathy Brice, embracing and all-smiles, dominated one wall.

"We are very sorry for your loss," Dani offered gently. "Has a family liaison officer been to see you yet?"

He shrugged his narrow shoulders. "I got a call a couple of days ago, but I put her off. I don't see how it would help." The man dropped onto the sofa.

"I know it doesn't seem that way now, but our FL officers are trained to help you through this terrible period." Dani decided to find the kitchen and make some teas. She'd leave Lawrence to the questioning, it was his jurisdiction after all.

The cups were hooked on a mug tree by the kettle. A box of teabags was easily identifiable in the cupboard above. The flat was small enough that she could hear the conversation taking place in the lounge.

Lawrence's tone was soft. "Could you describe what happened on the day Kathy was killed?"

There was a pause, almost as if the young man was composing himself before he finally spoke. "The morning routine was rushed, like it always is when Kathy's based at Heathrow."

"Where do you work, sir?"

"At a solicitor's firm near the Barbican. I've been there since I was a trainee. We both take the tube in the morning, so it's hectic. We just about managed a kiss goodbye."

"How did Kathy seem that day?"

"Completely normal. She showered and put on her uniform and then the makeup – they have to wear a lot of slap in that job. It's all about appearances. But Kathy didn't mind, she liked to dress up." His voice cracked.

"Did you have any contact with her for the remainder of the day?"

"Yes, we texted a few times during the lunchbreak. I was meant to shop for dinner on my way home, Kathy was telling me what to buy."

"We will need to look at those messages."

"Sure, I'm hardly likely to delete them. They're all

I've got now." The young man glanced up as Dani entered with a tray of mugs.

"Help yourself to milk and sugar," she offered.

Tom reached for one of the mugs, as if on automatic pilot. "Thanks. Tea is all I can stomach right now."

"When did you realise something was wrong?" Nate pressed.

"I got back with the shopping at around 6pm. I was expecting Kathy by half past at the latest. By 8.30pm I was getting frantic. I couldn't get any reply to her mobile. I'd called a couple of friends who she might possibly have stopped for a drink with on the way home, but they'd not seen her." He gingerly sipped the tea. "That's when you called me, DI Lawrence. You said you'd been expecting an email from Kathy that hadn't come. I told you she wasn't back from work yet, so you said you'd check with Lomond Airlines to see when she left. After that, I paced the flat until I got the call to say her body was found." He stared blankly out of the window. "It's like your entire life is turned upside down without warning."

"And you didn't leave this flat between receiving the call from DI Lawrence and being informed that Kathy was dead?"

He turned his head back to face the DCI. "No, of course not. I thought she could be home at any minute. I wanted to be here when she turned the key in the lock." Tears had now escaped onto his cheeks.

"Take a few moments, Mr Birch. Drink your tea."

He obediently took a couple more sips.

"Did Kathy enjoy working for Lomond?"

Tom blinked rapidly, seeming surprised by the question. "She loved the travel, and the passengers, most of the time. But Kathy did complain a bit about her work colleagues. I don't think she liked the boss much, either; thought he was a bit of a spiv. He was always trying to cut costs and bypass the unions. I said that was just how it was in that industry."

"Did she mention any colleague in particular she disliked? Someone she'd argued with, perhaps?"

He considered this. "Kathy really didn't warm to her new supervisor – the lady who came from BA. She said she was 'too big for her boots', or something like that." He shook his head sadly. "But you need to understand, that was just what Kathy was like. She enjoyed complaining about people, but it was harmless – she had a heart of gold, really." The tears were falling once more.

Dani spied a box of tissues on a side table and offered him one. "So, you wouldn't say Kathy had any enemies?"

Tom let out a grunt of frustration. "Why would she? Kathy was a normal young woman. We met in a bar when she was out with a group of mates and so was I. My girlfriend sometimes bitched about her work colleagues in the privacy of our own home. You find me anyone who hasn't been guilty of that?"

Nate nodded, the man had a point. "Thank you, Tom. We'll leave you in peace now. If I could take your mobile phone for the time being, I'd be most grateful. I promise it will be returned to you."

He got to his feet and reached for the phone in his back pocket. "Please find the person who did this, Inspector." His gaze was imploring.

Nate cleared his throat. "I promise I'll do everything I can."

*

They walked back to the car in silence. Dani knew her companion was deep in thought. When they were on the road back to the station in Hammersmith, Nate finally spoke. "When I had the phone conversation with Birch at 8.30pm, he was at home in Kilburn, but there is a chance he could have killed Kathy in the toilets at Heathrow and made it home by that time, especially if she was dead by 6pm, which is the coroner's earliest prediction."

Dani sighed. "We would have to get a DC to make the journey, to see if there was time, but I expect it's physically possible. What I'm not convinced about, is why Tom would want to kill his girlfriend. He clearly loved her. And how would he get into a security-controlled section of the airport?"

"Yep, I agree. We'll need to find out when he left work that afternoon. Maybe check his debit card to see where he did the shopping for dinner, get a time from the till-roll. Then we can rule him out as a suspect."

"Good. Because I'm feeling increasingly certain this was an inside job."

"At Lomond Airlines?"

"Yes. Tom insisted Kathy was a normal girl; bitching about colleagues like we all do in the comfort of our own homes. But I think Kathy somehow overstepped the mark. She complained about something that someone desperately wanted kept quiet. It was most likely to do with Autumn Carlisle."

Nate kept his gaze fixed on the road ahead, now mercifully clear of traffic. "Kathy had stumbled upon an incriminating piece of information and had a reputation for gossiping. When it was noted she'd started talking to us, this reputation got her killed."

Dani nodded sadly. She knew the DI was quite right.

Chapter 17

Trudy Gifford eagerly greeted the detectives on their return to the station. Her face was flushed from a surge of adrenaline. "I've been on the phone to Amsterdam, Boss. I finally got the go-ahead from the Chief Commissioner over there to question our Dutch witnesses."

Nate gestured for his DC to take a seat at her workstation where he and Dani pulled up chairs to join her. "Go ahead, Trudy. Fill us in."

"I spoke with Lucas and Sofie Vos at their flat in the east of the city. We got a Skype connection and I recorded the conversation."

"This was the couple who were friends of Autumn Carlisle?" Dani leant forward with interest.

Trudy nodded. "They didn't know of Autumn's death until the local police got in touch with them, asking for permission for us to question them. The case hadn't reached the news over there."

"If they weren't next of kin, there's no reason why they should have been notified," Nate added, without a hint of defensiveness.

"No, but the pair were very shocked and upset, I could see that. They met Autumn about seven years ago, when she bought a piece of artwork from them. They went out to lunch to celebrate the sale and remained firm friends. Lucas and Sofie had dinner with Autumn in the week before she died."

"During her short-haul trip to Amsterdam?" Dani ran a hand through her hair. "How did Autumn seem to them on that occasion?"

"Sofie said they were worried about her. Autumn had seemed in lower spirits than normal. They put it down to her being single again. Sofie had suggested she try Internet dating, but Autumn had dismissed the idea out of hand, said she was too busy in her new job for a relationship. Lucas interrupted his wife to remind her that Autumn had expressed concern about her mother."

"Betsy Carlisle?" Dani's interest was piqued.

"Yes, Lucas said Autumn's mum had some long-standing mental-health issues. Mrs Carlisle was prone to bouts of extreme anxiety and insomnia. During their last dinner, Autumn had said she'd always assumed her mother's condition was something unique to her. But now, she wondered whether it might be hereditary."

"Mental health issues certainly can run in families," Nate added, "I wonder why Autumn was only just considering the possibility now?"

Dani crinkled her brow. "Because this was the first time in her life that she'd ever experienced those kinds of symptoms. Her father mentioned it when I spoke with him in Glasgow. Autumn had been having bad dreams in the months leading up to her death. These visions filled her with a sense of dread. Perhaps she thought she was inheriting her mother's mental-health condition?"

Nate frowned. "This theory lends credence to our original assumption of suicide. Did the couple tell you anything else? Had Autumn fallen out with someone here in London? Was she frightened something bad might happen to her?"

Trudy crossed her arms over her chest. "You can watch the recording in full, Boss. Lucas and Sophie only talk about Autumn's state of mind. They didn't get the impression there was anyone significant in the woman's life outside of work and family. But they got the distinct impression she wasn't happy."

Dani leant back in her chair and allowed her gaze to slide up to the tiled ceiling, noticing a couple of brownish stains by the light-fitting. "If she didn't confide in her closest friends, maybe there was nothing to tell? Perhaps Autumn was simply spiralling into a suicidal depression inherited from her mother?"

Nate shook his head violently. "I know I thought that way at first, but things have changed now. Kathy Brice's murder spins that theory on its head."

The certainty in the DI's tone brought Dani up short. "Okay, let's accept there's something deeper going on here. I still think we need to find out more about Betsy Carlisle's condition. She kept that very quiet when she first approached my friend, Professor Morgan."

"I'm not surprised," Nate scoffed. "Autumn's parents were trying to persuade your mate that their daughter's death wasn't due to suicide, despite all the physical evidence at the time, suggesting this was the case. They were hardly going to openly supply the information that her mother suffered from a serious mental health condition that could well be hereditary."

"I suppose not. I'll need to make a few calls to Scotland." Dani was lost in her thoughts.

"You can use my office for a bit of privacy," Nate added.

Trudy was tapping information into her laptop. "There's something else, too."

"Oh, yes?"

"Autumn's ex-boyfriend, Noel Colbert, informed me of an incident from her past. He said there would be a police record of it." She finished tapping and slid the device round so the screen faced her colleagues.

Dani scanned the text, as Trudy provided a précis. "In the Summer of 2011, when Autumn was a young stewardess, straight out of college, she was a member of the flight crew on a BA passenger jet to Sharm El Sheikh in Egypt. A lone male passenger was on the flight. His name was Austin Johnson, 28 years old at the time. According to a statement Autumn made to police on her return to England, Johnson paid her a great deal of attention during the flight. He was very talkative and ordered a lot of drinks, a number of his comments were suggestive and inappropriate. When they arrived in Egypt, Autumn and the rest of the crew were staying at a hotel near the airport. Ms Carlisle claimed that Johnson must have followed her off the flight and found out where she was staying."

"A stalker?" Nate added.

"Seems like it. Then, on her second night in Egypt, Autumn reported that a man, who she identified as Austin Johnson, followed her during an evening walk from her hotel to an area of bars and restaurants where she was planning to eat an evening meal. He accosted her on a quiet street, pushing her into undergrowth nearby and sexually assaulting her."

Dani read the details of the attack. "Autumn was groped and man-handled, it seems Johnson was attempting a rape, but she managed to scream and attract the attention of passers-by. Johnson ran off."

Trudy continued. "Autumn claimed she was so shocked by the incident, she didn't report it until she returned to the UK. She crewed a return flight the next day, trying to force the attack from her mind."

"What happened to Johnson?" Nate's forehead was furrowed with concern.

"He denied the charges, claimed he was in a

resort in Sharm El Sheikh when the attack occurred. A couple of waitresses backed-up his story, said they'd served him dinner that night. The police had to drop the charge of attempted rape. But there were plenty of witnesses willing to make statements about Johnson's harassing behaviour on the flight. So, he was cautioned for being drunk and disorderly and banned from travelling on BA planes for two years."

Dani shook her head. "It doesn't seem like much of a punishment."

Nate shrugged. "It sounds like there wasn't enough evidence for the UK police to take the assault charge further. It must have shaken Autumn up badly though, she was very young when it happened."

Dani nodded her agreement. "Is it not odd for a young, single man to take a package holiday on his own?"

Trudy grimaced. "I'd say so, but there's no law against it."

"No, there isn't, but I'd certainly like to know what this Austin Johnson fellow is up to now," Nate added in a steely tone.

"I'll get onto it straightaway, Boss," Trudy replied, turning her laptop back round the right way and determinedly punching the keys.

Chapter 18

The afternoon sun was hot as Rhodri approached the entrance to the Pitt Street Station. The professor wondered how warm it must be down in London if it was so sultry here in Glasgow. He imagined Dani probably wasn't having much of an opportunity to enjoy it, anyway. He felt a pang of guilt at this, knowing her involvement in the London murders were ultimately his responsibility.

A helpful PC at the reception desk led Rhodri to one of the interview rooms on the ground floor. He didn't usually have to pass through so many formalities when making a visit to the Serious Crime Division.

He sat patiently, a cup of weak tea placed on the worn table in front of him. Finally, the door opened. A man with a slick of dark hair and a neat suit entered the room.

"Good afternoon, Professor Morgan. My name is DI Dermot Muir."

"I'm pleased to meet you, Inspector. DCI Bevan instructed me to get in touch with you."

He nodded. "Yes, I spoke with her yesterday. She has updated me on the Carlisles' connection to the case she is investigating in London."

Rhodri assessed the young man seated before him. "I thought I might be able to liaise with DS Calder? Is he not available today?"

Dermot gave a thin, tolerant smile. "DS Calder is involved in another investigation right now. I'm the acting senior officer in the division. It's appropriate for you to work with me on this."

"Oh, of course, I wasn't suggesting you weren't of

sufficient rank to assist me, it's just I'm used to working with DCI Bevan, DS Calder and DI Mann. We have an established professional rapport."

Dermot had to resist making a sarcastic comment. "Well, Alice is on maternity leave and I am her replacement, so I will have to do for now." He took a breath and flicked on his tablet computer. "So, what can you tell me about Betsy Carlisle?"

Rhodri brought a tatty, bulging file out of his briefcase. "I've never been Betsy's practitioner, you understand. I was only told about her mental health issues a few days ago. I always knew she could be 'nervy', but that's a long way from being a clinical case."

Dermot nodded, hoping the man with the wayward snowy hair opposite him would eventually get to the point.

"I rang Mike Carlisle yesterday. He agreed to supply me with the notes that various psychiatrists have made on Betsy over the years. I drove to Cumbernauld this morning to pick it up."

Dermot laid his hand on the file. "Will a layman be able to understand the information in here?"

Rhodri nodded enthusiastically. "I spent about an hour scanning through the information before I got here. It's pretty straightforward stuff. Betsy has undergone courses of CBT and has been on mood stabilising medication for about a decade. Until the death of her daughter she was entirely stable."

"Cognitive Behavioural Therapy?" Dermot asked tentatively.

"That's right!" Rhodri beamed, as if praising a star pupil. "You see, it's perfectly possible for a non-practitioner to follow the notes. The *man on the street* is much more clued-up on issues of mental health than they would have been a decade ago."

"In the case of Betsy Carlisle, are we talking

about a serious psychological condition? Is she suffering from some kind of psychosis? Might she have had hallucinations, or suicidal thoughts?"

Rhodri considered this carefully. "I'd need more time to analysis these notes fully, but I'd say her case displays fairly typical evidence of a moderate nervous condition, at times exacerbated by stress. There is no suggestion here of psychosis. I certainly never detected such symptoms in Autumn."

"But you'd not seen as much of your friends' daughter in recent years?"

Rhodri sighed. "No, that is correct."

Dermot nodded with resolution. "I'll get a copy made of the file and bike it over to you. Then we can both read through it and see what we think?"

Rhodri narrowed his bright blue eyes. "I thought I knew Betsy and Mike well. We'd been friends for years. But when we last met, they mentioned some aspects of their life I'd never known about."

"Such as?" Dermot enquired.

"Well, Betsy's illness for a start. You'd have thought they'd have shared it with me earlier – I *am* a highly regarded practitioner in the field after all."

"Perhaps that's exactly why they didn't."

Rhodri nodded in solemn agreement. "Yes, I can see that."

"But there was something else they kept from you?"

Rhodri snapped out of his reverie. "Yes, Betsy mentioned she'd been abroad for a while, before Autumn was born. When they were back in Scotland together and had their daughter, they were living in the Highlands. I never knew that about them. I was always discussing my academic postings abroad, when I was still with my wife and the boys were young. My life was an open book to them."

"It's something I could look into; the Carlisle's

past addresses must be easy enough to find on the database. But to be honest, professor, I'm not sure how it would connect to their daughter's death? Autumn Carlisle was killed down in London. The DCI seems to reckon it had something to do with her job at the airline. I don't see how her parents' lifestyle choices several decades ago can have much of a bearing on it?"

Rhodri shook his head of unruly hair and tutted in self-admonishment. "You're quite correct, of course. I shouldn't let my own vanity affect my judgement. The Carlisles clearly held back certain aspects of their lives from me, as is their prerogative." He stood abruptly, the plastic chair scraping across the tiled floor behind him. "I'll be awaiting the arrival of the file, Inspector. Then I will give the notes my full attention."

Dermot rose to see the professor out of the station, thinking what an odd character he seemed to be.

Chapter 19

The departure gate was busy. An aircraft on the tarmac outside was ready to board. The sun was beating through the tall glass windows. Dani felt the sweat tingle between her shoulder blades.

"Is this the right place?" The DCI had been to the scene of Kathy Brice's murder once before, but she found the endless carpeted corridors and waiting areas all looked the same.

"Yep, it's number 52," Nate replied confidently.

Dani glanced at one of the screens suspended from the ceiling. "This plane is heading for Rome."

"On the afternoon of Kathy's murder, a Lomond Airways flight to Ciampino Airport in Rome, had departed at 5.45pm. But by 6pm, her estimated time of death, the area would have been quiet. The next flight wasn't scheduled to leave until after 8pm."

"What about the flight manifest for the quarter to six departure? Did it reveal any names of interest?"

"According to the print-out we were given, there were 32 passengers on the flight. There were a handful of families, several single fliers and a few business people. Rome isn't a typical destination for a package holiday, it's more a city-break kind of location."

The screen above them began to flash and the passengers seated nearby gravitated to form a long line in front of a desk, where a Lomond Airlines representative in a smart uniform was examining their travel documents. Nate moved over to take one of the vacated sofas. He gestured for Dani to join him.

The DI summoned up a list of names on the

screen of his phone. "These are the people who were in this lounge on the afternoon Kathy was killed. Trudy has contacted them all, none has a connection to the victim. The cabin crew on the aircraft that day didn't notice anyone acting oddly either before or during the flight."

Dani chewed her bottom lip. "What about Kathy herself? How often had she worked out of this particular departure gate?"

Nate deftly flicked to another screen. "Three times in the past year. She tended to work on short-haul flights, so this one featured on her schedule. But she didn't use it any more than any other on her itinerary."

Dani sighed. "There doesn't seem to be any good reason for Kathy to come down here on the day she was killed."

As the snaking line of passengers slowly disappeared through the boarding gate, the waiting area fell eerily quiet.

Dani glanced at the screen. "There's not another departure for an hour." She gazed around her at the area, now devoid of people. "It must have been like this when Kathy went into the toilets. No wonder there are no witnesses."

Nate tutted as he observed the clutter of cardboard coffee cups and crisp packets that had been left on the tables by the sofas. He was about to sweep them into the bin when the creak of a trolley signalled the approach of one of the cleaning staff, making a beeline for gate 52.

Dani shot her colleague a meaningful glance. "The cleaning team must be primed to arrive after a gate has cleared of passengers. They must tidy away their detritus before the next lot arrive."

Nate got to his feet as a middle-aged man in a blue overall, pushing a trolley stacked with brushes and mops reached them. He brought out his warrant card. "We're investigating the suspicious death of a Lomond Airline employee that occurred here on late Wednesday afternoon last week. Did you happen to be on duty at the time?"

The man furrowed his brow. When he spoke, his accent was eastern European. "I was working on the main concourse when it happened. Some of my colleagues were questioned by the airport police about it. I think it was Margaritte who was on duty in this area when the girl was killed." He scratched his head. "She saw nothing, mind you." He threw his hand up to indicate the length of the glass-flanked corridor. "We cover a wide area. She wasn't anywhere near the toilets when it happened." The man pulled on a plastic glove and began depositing the rubbish in a bin bag, a sign he had no more to add.

Nate nodded. "Thank you for your time."

The detectives made their way towards the exit. "So much for thinking we may have stumbled upon a witness."

Dani shot him a look. "There may not have been an airport cleaner in the area when Kathy was killed, but it might explain how our murderer was able to move about unchallenged in a high-security area."

Nate stopped walking. "If he or she was dressed like a cleaner, you mean?"

Dani shrugged. "It's possible. If a cleaner entered the toilets after Kathy, she probably wouldn't have been suspicious about their presence."

"It's definitely worth checking out. The staff who work on this side of passport control must have identity passes and have undergone rigorous security checks."

"But if someone possesses the right equipment and looks the part, is anyone going to scrutinise their credentials that hard?"

Nate squared his broad shoulders. "I'll have a word with the airport security manager. If your theory is correct, our perp may appear on CCTV images from other areas of the airport. If their appearance doesn't match photos from current personnel files, we've got our killer."

Dani sighed. "But that's one hell of a job. Heathrow covers thousands of square feet, if our perp was a pro, they'd know how to obscure their features when passing a camera. If it was me, I'd wear a baseball cap."

Nate shrugged. "Well, right now it's our only lead for Kathy Brice's murder. If my boss allows me more man-power I think it's worth a try."

*

Denny Lomond's secretary, Diane Martin, was talking to the detectives whilst she arranged envelopes on her desk. She appeared stressed. "We have our own cleaning personnel, but they work only on our aeroplanes. All airport areas are covered by Heathrow."

"Might one of your cleaners have clearance to enter the main airport? Could they gain access to secure areas?"

Diane finally glanced up. "I wouldn't have thought so. Our domestic staff have different uniforms to the ones used at Heathrow. We live in a post 9/11 world, Inspector. Airport security is extremely tight."

Yet, Nate knew that human error was always a possibility, even with the strongest security. The focus at airports was always placed on passengers rather than staff. Uniforms had an uncanny ability to make people invisible.

Dani stepped forward. "We will need a list of your cleaning staff, along with their contact details."

Diane sighed theatrically. "I'll let the Operations Manager know, he's got a database of information. He is extremely efficient." She had begun stuffing letters into the envelopes.

"Mr Lomond is keeping you busy, I see?" Nate commented lightly, knowing this would annoy the secretary.

"I'm *always* busy, Inspector. But on top of my usual duties, I also find myself at the sharp end of an industrial dispute. These letters set out the final pay agreement with our pilots." She threw her hands up in the air. "Let's hope it sees an end to all this nonsense."

"Are the cabin crew involved in these negotiations at all?" Dani enquired, genuinely interested. "Didn't they have any issues over pay or conditions?"

"No, thank God. We could certainly do without that on top of everything else." She met Dani's eye for the first time. "Autumn Carlisle was a good appointment in that respect. As a manager, she kept Mr Lomond very well informed about the needs of her crew. If there were any complaints, she would have told us about it before things ever reached a crisis point. Unlike this current mess with the pilots. I just hope her replacement will be as capable."

"Did Ms Carlisle spend a lot of time with Mr Lomond, then?" Nate kept his tone neutral.

"She came to his office once a week, on a Friday morning at 10am. I made a pot of coffee and brought in some nice pastries from the French café on the concourse. Mr Lomond insisted on it."

"Did you ever suspect their relationship was more than just professional?"

Diane dropped the envelope she was filling and looked surprised. "Not at all. They worked well together, but I never thought it was anything more than that."

"Before she was killed, Kathy Brice suggested to us there was more to the relationship, that Autumn may have been sleeping with Denny Lomond."

Diane rolled her eyes. "Well, I don't wish to speak ill of the dead, but that girl was quite a gossip. I don't tend to be 'in the loop' myself, being up here in Mr Lomond's office most of the time, but a couple of the stewardesses told me in the canteen that Kathy was," she cleared her throat awkwardly. "A *shit-stirrer*, was the exact term they used."

Dani smiled thinly at the expression, which didn't sit easily on Diane's lips. "We heard similar accusations during our interviews. But it doesn't mean Kathy wasn't sometimes correct in her theories."

The secretary took a step back from the desk, as if she'd been given an electric shock, her customary composure briefly slipping. "Yes, I suppose that's right."

*

Nate followed the slow traffic as it inched out of the short-stay airport car-park. "My team have got plenty of work to do. The airport police are releasing the digital recordings from thirty different surveillance cameras that were operating last Wednesday."

"You'll also have the list of Lomond's cleaning staff by the end of today."

Nate grunted. "You don't fancy inviting some of your staff down from Glasgow to join the party, do you?"

Dani laughed. She thought about Andy Calder and how he would be reacting to having Dermot Muir in temporary charge of the department. For a split second, she was tempted. "I don't think it would wash with my DCS. But I've got a couple of people back home taking a look at Autumn's mother for us."

"Yeah, I do appreciate that." He gripped the steering wheel and gave an awkward grin. "I know you're staying in that crappy travel hotel. I'd hate to think you were considering heading back north yourself. To be honest, I need your help on this case."

"I must admit, the food in the hotel bar could be better."

Nate swivelled in his seat. "You're welcome to kip at my place. I've got a spare room that never gets used. I don't cook, but you could have full use of my kitchen."

Dani smiled. "I'm grateful for the offer, but I promise you I'm quite comfortable where I am. You don't have to worry, I'm as determined to solve this case as you are."

He looked relieved. "As long as you're here, the bosses won't take this out of my hands. I reckon my DCI thinks I'm out of my depth. He's constantly checking up on my progress."

"It's your case, Nate. I'm just assisting. Try to have more confidence in your policing." Dani was irritated that she'd managed to end up bolstering the DI's ego again. She resolved to say no more on the subject.

"Right, I'll drop you off at your hotel on the way back to Hammersmith. It's been a long day, try to get a decent night's sleep."

Dani relaxed back into the passenger seat, watching the dense traffic flowing on either side of them. She liked DI Lawrence, he was a compassionate and clever cop. But on a personal level, she wouldn't deny he could be extremely hard work.

Chapter 20

Dani was woken in the early hours of the morning by the low rumble she had come to recognise as the first jets of the day landing at Heathrow. The hotel staff kept telling her it was something one grew used to, but the noise still grated on Dani's nerves.

For a few moments, when Dani's body felt heavy with a yearning for more sleep, she briefly considered Nate's offer of the use of his spare room. Was his flat in the flight path of the airport, she wondered? She quickly quashed these thoughts as it dawned on her she'd almost certainly be required to provide him with a daily pep-talk on his abilities as a police detective.

Instead of dwelling on the prospect, Dani took a shower and woke herself up with a strong coffee from the hotel's buffet breakfast. Knowing that Nate's team would be tied up with the CCTV footage from the airport all day, she had requested the personal use of an unmarked car.

When the officer from Hammersmith handed over the keys to a silver Mondeo estate in the hotel car-park, it wasn't yet 8am. Dani took advantage of the clear roads to set the coordinates for Haywards Heath, West Sussex into the sat nav.

The sun was rising over the undulating countryside as Dani drove out of the urban sprawl of south London. There wasn't a cloud in the sky. It was obviously going to be another hot day. A haze of warm air already hung over the tarmac of the road ahead, a phenomenon which rarely occurred back home in Scotland.

It was just after nine when Dani entered the town and scoured the road signs for directions to a car-park. She found one near the centre and displayed a ticket that gave her a couple of hours to look around.

Dani knew Haywards Heath was the nearest town to the village of Mitchling, where Autumn Carlisle had lived for several years. She imagined the air stewardess would have spent a reasonable amount of time here. It would have been where she'd have used the supermarket and got petrol, picked up her prescriptions from the chemist, perhaps.

The High Street was an attractive mix of old and new buildings. The place had the air of confident affluence to it. Dani stopped when she reached a café which was displaying local art and crafts in the window. She recalled Autumn buying a piece of art from the couple in Amsterdam and decided to go inside.

The café had only just opened. The smell of freshly baked produce made Dani's stomach grumble. She'd only had a coffee for breakfast. A small, balding man in a green apron beamed at her from the other side of the counter.

Dani ordered a cappuccino and a home-made Danish pastry, lingering to examine the paintings on the walls whilst her order was prepared. Most of the images rendered within the neat, white frames were of the lush, gentle hills and skies of the South Downs, or the coastline which lay not far beyond. Dani paused when she saw a collection of watercolours depicting light aircraft; some of which were on the ground and others looping amongst fluffy clouds; all had been executed by a skilful hand.

The man in the apron carried over the cappuccino and pastry on a tiny tray, placing them on the table nearest Dani. "They're very good, aren't they?" He commented affably.

"Yes, they are. Is the artist local?"

The man stood still and folded his arms across a portly chest. "The ones of the planes are by Arthur Keating. He lives in one of the nearby villages. He used to fly in the RAF, but he's long retired. Those paintings are of the light aircraft out at Colville."

Dani looked bemused. "What's Colville?"

"Oh, it's an airfield. We've got a fair few in the area. We're not just about Gatwick and the big Airbuses, you know."

Dani sipped her coffee and took a bite of pastry; it was crumbly, buttery and delicious. "I've spent quite a bit of time at big airports recently. To be honest, I could do without seeing another one for a while."

"Frequent overseas traveller, are you?"

Dani nodded with her mouth full, not wanting to have to explain.

"We have a lot of air crew who live here in town. They take the bus into Gatwick. It brings money to the area without a doubt and business to us cafés and restaurants. But the countryside is lovely. We dread the airport expanding like it will at Heathrow, although it feels like just a matter of time for us." He sighed heavily.

Dani sat up straighter in her seat. "Do you know a lady called Autumn Carlisle? She had a cottage in Mitchling and probably came into the town a lot. She was a stewardess for BA."

The man wrinkled his brow. "I don't know the name, I'm sorry."

Dani fumbled in her bag for a copy of the photo of Autumn from her Lomond Airlines employee file. She folded it out flat and showed it to the man.

He examined it carefully. "Goodness, yes. I know that lady. She has the most gorgeous red hair and was always beautifully made-up. I should have known she was an air stewardess." He smiled wistfully. "But she's not been in for over a year, at least."

Dani felt her heart beat quicken. "Was she a regular customer?"

"Not like the folk who come in everyday for their cuppa. She was perhaps here once or twice a month. But like you, she was very interested in our artwork." He narrowed his eyes. "In fact, I'm pretty sure she bought one of Arthur's paintings. I recall it because I was surprised at her choice."

"Why was that?"

"It wasn't one of the pictures showing the aircraft in flight. I thought the piece she chose was rather dark. It was of a light aircraft that had crashed into woodland. There were no dead bodies in it, or anything gruesome like that. But the plane itself almost had the appearance of a dead animal; mangled and lifeless." He shuddered. "I certainly wouldn't have had it on my wall at home."

Dani gulped down the last of her coffee. "Do you have the contact details for Arthur Keating?"

"Of course. He comes in every few weeks to replace the pictures that have sold and collect his payments." The café owner reached across to the shelf beneath the paintings. "Better still, why don't you take one of his business cards? It's got all of his details on."

Dani pocketed the card gratefully. She opened her wallet to pay for what she'd had, resolving to leave a generous tip on top.

*

On her way to Arthur Keating's address, Dani passed the sign for Colville Airfield. With the windows down on the deserted country lane, she could hear the puttering of one of the small aircraft passing overhead.

The Sat Nav instructed her to turn off the road and onto a rough single track. Dani grimaced as the car bumped over the loose stones, she could only hope the silver paintwork didn't end up chipped.

Eventually, the track halted at a substantial stone house. She parked up and approached the front door. Despite ringing the bell several times, there was no reply. A relatively new 4x4 sat in the driveway next to the house, so Dani was reasonably confident there was somebody on the property.

She trudged towards an outhouse connected to a set of garages. It had what looked like a newly installed chimney poking out of the corrugated roof. The door was open, but Dani knocked confidently on it before entering, calling out, "is anybody home?"

"Come in, I'm just working on a tricky section." An elderly male voice floated out from somewhere inside.

Dani took a few steps forward. The interior of the outhouse had been converted into a large studio. A huge wood burning stove was positioned in the centre of the space. Canvases were propped up against every beam.

A tall, delicately built man in paint flecked shirt and jeans was standing with his back to Dani. He was applying brush strokes to a painting on an easel which was catching the light streaming through a Velux window.

"Mr Keating? My name is DCI Dani Bevan. I'm a detective with the Glasgow police."

Keating instantly put down his brush and turned to face his visitor. Able to view his features, Dani placed him as in his mid-seventies.

"A *Detective Chief Inspector* from Scotland. Well, well, to what do I owe this honour?"

Dani felt a little awkward. Her jurisdiction in this area was disputable and her reasons for questioning this man were speculative at best. "I'm in London assisting the police with an investigation. A woman died in suspicious circumstances at her Hillingdon flat two weeks back. But before a few months ago, the lady had been a resident in Mitchling. She worked as a stewardess for BA. I believe she once bought a painting from you?"

Keating took a step forward. "Miss Carlisle?" His narrow mouth parted in shock. "She's dead?"

"I'm afraid so. Did you know her well?"

Keating moved over to a bench which lined one wall of the studio. He lifted across a couple of mugs and filled them from a jug attached to a coffee machine. "Would you like a drink?"

"Yes please."

"There's milk in the jug," the man stated absently, gesturing to a tray with various pieces of crockery on it. "I wouldn't say I knew Autumn well. As you say, she bought a painting from me. Usually, I have nothing to do with the folk who buy my art from Glen's café. But this lady had taken a card along with her purchase and she contacted me."

Dani sipped the coffee, it was only lukewarm but very good. "Did you meet her?"

Keating nodded. "She wrote me a letter, in what must have been the Spring of 2017. Miss Carlisle had recently bought 'Eagle'; a painting I had made of a light aircraft which crashed into the woods behind the house about five years back. Eagle was the name of the plane."

"The crash occurred near here?" Dani automatically glanced around her.

"You may have noticed as you arrived, that the airfield is only a mile or so to the east?"

"Yes, I saw the sign."

"I was awoken one foggy morning by the terrible sound of a plane coming down into the forest which backs onto my garden. I dressed quickly and ran out to search for the wreckage. I knew it was only a matter of time before the thing went up in flames."

Dani sipped her coffee in silence, allowing him to continue.

"I smelt the smoke before I saw the crash site. The pilot was badly injured, he was slumped against the door of the cockpit. I used a branch to lever the thing open and dragged him out. We got clear just before the fuel went up."

"Was the pilot okay?"

Keating's face was solemn. "He broke his neck. The plane had only just taken off when the nose clipped the tops of the trees which must have been obscured by the fog. Any higher and his injuries would have undoubtedly been fatal. I believe his mobility has returned to a certain extent, but he still requires a wheelchair to get about."

At least he didn't burn to death, trapped in his own plane, Dani thought but didn't say.

"The whole incident had a profound effect upon me. I was in the RAF myself for a time. I was already painting planes as a hobby."

"What made you paint the wreckage?"

He sighed. "Some might find it morbid, I suppose. For me, it was therapeutic. After the fire had burnt itself out, the lump of twisted metal seemed to have taken on the form of a wounded animal. It was almost like a sculpture had been placed amongst the charred trunks of the trees, having melded itself into the organic matter which enclosed it. I found myself sketching the image before the authorities arrived to clear it away."

"It seems like an odd choice of subject for Autumn to buy. She spent half her life in planes, I'm surprised she'd want to look at a crashed one."

Keating opened a drawer in an old metal filing cabinet near his easel. "This might help to explain it to you." He handed over an envelope.

"Is this Autumn's letter to you?"

"Yes. In it, she explains how much the painting had affected her. She asks to meet up with me, to find out the story behind it. I invited her here to my studio to talk. She only lived in Mitchling, just a ten-minute drive away." Keating put down his mug. "Come on Detective Chief Inspector, I'll show you what I showed Miss Carlisle on the day she came."

Chapter 21

Inside the forest, under the canopy of wide green leaves, the heat of the day receded dramatically. Arthur Keating led Dani along a meandering path until the gate leading into the garden at the rear of his stone house was no longer visible.

The dense line of trees abruptly parted and a break in the forest appeared. The tall trunks were unnaturally bowed. The ground was dusty and grey, without the covering of verdant mosses and humus which populated the rest of the forest floor. The sun had found a gap here. Its rays shone mercilessly on their heads. It was eerily silent, as if the wildlife kept their distance from the place.

"The vegetation never fully recovered from the fire. I suppose if I raked out all traces of the ash and debris it might have a chance of rejuvenation. It's just so difficult to get any proper equipment down here."

Dani touched the bark of one of the trees, it crumbled to a blackened dust in her hand. "Why was Autumn Carlisle so keen to see the site of the crash?"

"She said my painting had a profound effect upon her. She saw it hanging on the wall in the café and was mesmerised. Miss Carlisle believed she'd seen something very like it herself, but she couldn't recall where. I think she hoped that coming here might release the memory."

"Did it?"

Keating scratched his head. "I'm not sure. She walked around the clearing for a while. I left her alone, returning to the house to brew coffee. She came back to join me when she was ready."

"Did she speak about anything else?"

"We discussed her job and my artwork, but it was small talk really. I sensed she'd seen what she came to. We shook hands at the front door, and I watched her drive away. I heard nothing from her after that. I'd not even heard her name mentioned until you came here today." Keating turned to face Dani. "Can you tell me how she died?"

There was a sadness in Keating's voice but also a practicality. Dani sensed this was a man who had grown accustomed to death. "Miss Carlisle was found in her flat with her wrists cut. At first, we assumed it was suicide, but further evidence has made us suspect foul play."

Keating switched his gaze back to the clearing. "I only met her that once, but I don't believe she was the type to kill herself. Autumn struck me as a survivor. Like me, she had witnessed the horror of a plane crash, even though she may not have been able to fully recall it. She'd also recognised the odd beauty of its aftermath."

Dani wasn't sure she completely understood.

"It isn't something I'm proud of. I know the risks of aviation; the terrible consequences when things go wrong. I've lost friends to it. but I still find it beguiling and wonderful."

Dani nodded, feeling suddenly unsettled in their surroundings.

"Let's go back to the house and I'll make a proper brew of coffee – piping hot this time."

"Thank you, that would be much appreciated." Dani followed Keating back onto the path, striding towards the little gate without once glancing back.

*

The village of Mitchling looked like a picture postcard in the sun's afternoon glow. Dani thought about James and how much he would like it there for a weekend away. They would take a stroll to the old church and maybe have a pub lunch at the King's Arms. Today, she was only interested in Autumn Carlisle.

She drove along the lane until she reached Maple cottage, pulling up on the grass verge opposite. When Dani got out of the car, she saw Mrs Forbes on her knees in the front garden, a wide-brimmed hat propped on top of her sculpted silver hair, her gloved hand stabbing at the soil with a trowel, the other squarely on the ground, keeping her upright.

The woman glanced up from her labours as Dani approached the gate. The little black poodle began scampering in circles on the grass. She leant on a wooden bench to lever herself to standing. "You are one of the detectives who visited me the other day! I'm sorry, I can't recall your name."

"DCI Bevan. Please don't let me interrupt your gardening."

"Oh. It's alright. I can't bend over for too long, as it is." Mrs Forbes eyed Dani carefully. "Is there any news about poor Miss Carlisle?"

"Nothing significant yet. I just wondered if Miss Carlisle left any artwork here? We've recently discovered she possessed a painting from a local artist, but it wasn't hanging in her London flat."

Mrs Forbes put her hands on her hips and stretched her back. "Actually, there's still a heap of old junk in the shed in the back garden. I rarely go out there because the bloody trees make it so dark and dingy. I'm still waiting for the men to come and chop them down."

"Do you mind if I go and have a look?"

"Not at all. Come into the kitchen through the

back door when you've finished. There's a jug of lemonade on the table."

Dani nodded her thanks and made her way around the side of the cottage to the back garden. She stared up at the maple trees which were indeed completely obscuring the sun. They towered above the cottage and did seem disproportionate when compared to the modest size of the property.

The shed was in a corner of the plot, the bushes around it overgrown and thick with brambles. Dani turned the handle and stepped inside. The smell of damp filled her nostrils. Underneath a loosely laid tarpaulin was a cardboard box full of books. Dani rifled through the paperbacks. There was nothing of any great interest; a few Penguin classics and modern crime novels, all with curled corners and yellowing pages.

Leaning against the box were a collection of framed pictures. It didn't take long for Dani to find the one she was looking for. Fortunately, Arthur Keating had used a decent glass frame for his painting, otherwise, sitting out there in the damp conditions, it would have been ruined.

She tucked 'Eagle' under her arm and scanned the remaining contents of the shed. There were a couple of beautiful wood carvings on a shelf; one was of an owl and the other looked like a wolf. They were obviously produced by a skilful craftsperson.

Dani pulled the door shut firmly behind her, shivering as she marched up the lawn, slipping through the back door into the pretty cottage kitchen. She was gasping for that glass of lemonade. Mrs Forbes must have heard her enter, as the lady promptly emerged from the sitting room with an inquisitive expression on her face.

"Any luck, Detective?"

Dani held up the painting. "This is the one I was

looking for. Do you mind if I take it back to the station in London?"

Mrs Forbes nodded vigorously. "Of course, it belonged to Autumn, not me." She stepped forward to examine it more closely. "Oh dear, the subject matter isn't very cheerful, is it?"

"No," Dani agreed between gulps of lemonade.

"I prefer paintings of dogs and flowers myself."

Dani smiled. "But you should take a good look at the stuff out there in the shed. There are a couple of wood carvings of animals that are lovely. It seems a shame to hide them away."

The lady looked intrigued. "Oh yes, I shall. It seems Miss Carlisle was full of surprises."

Dani raised her eyebrows archly, she couldn't help but agree.

Chapter 22

Nate leaned out from behind the computer screen and gave the object tucked under Dani's arm a curious glance. "What the hell is that?"

Dani chuckled. "It's a painting that belonged to Autumn. She'd left it at Maple Cottage when she moved to Hillingdon. I think it may have some significance."

The DI shrugged his shoulders. "Fair enough. I've got five officers trawling through this CCTV footage." He swung his long legs out from beneath the desk and gave them a stretch. "A *lot* of people come and go through Heathrow each day. We're talking thousands."

Dani could imagine the sheer scale of the task before them. The process had the potential to take weeks. "How many cleaning personnel can you pick out of the crowds?"

"Oh, plenty. But it's like you said, being able to identify them clearly enough to match their faces to the employee files is near enough impossible. Most of the time they've got their heads down mopping the floors."

"Maybe this isn't the strongest line of enquiry we could pursue?" Dani's tone was thoughtful.

Nate threw his hands up. "Then suggest me another one, I'd love to hear it!"

Before Dani could answer, Trudy approached her boss's desk. She slapped a piece of paper down on it triumphantly. "The current address of Mr Austin Johnson, the man who sexually harassed Autumn Carlisle on a flight to Egypt in 2011."

Nate swung forward and clutched for the details.

"Great work, Trudy."

"Johnson is now 36 years old and works as a salesman for a home improvement company in Woking."

Nate looked at his watch. "Do you fancy paying him a visit?" He tipped his head in Dani's direction. "I'll treat you to dinner afterwards?"

Dani felt exhausted after her day of driving, but she sensed Nate was full of energy, like a coiled spring, after his lengthy shift behind a computer screen. "Sure, why not? As long as we take your car."

Nate leapt to his feet. "Of course, any excuse to get behind the wheel."

*

The sun was finally setting as Nate eased his Mercedes onto the driveway of the suburban semi in Woking, where there was just enough room for it beside a bulky SUV.

"Seems like someone's at home." Nate led the way to the front door.

A plump, pretty woman in her thirties answered swiftly, she was holding a tea towel in her hand. "Oh, what can I do for you?"

Nate held up his warrant card. "We're looking for Mr Austin Johnson."

She appeared taken aback. "Austin's my husband. He will be in the shed round the side of the house, fixing his bike."

The detectives left her on the doorstep staring blankly after them. The lean-to was beyond an unlocked gate and attached to the kitchen. The door was propped open. A man could be seen kneeling down beside an up-turned bicycle, his hands smeared with grease.

He turned sharply as he heard them approach. "Who are you?" He demanded.

As Nate introduced himself for a second time, Dani took in the man's appearance. Austin Johnson was tall and broad. He had a full head of thick, dark hair. When he reached for a cloth and rubbed his beefy hands clean of grease, Dani felt reminded of someone.

"What's this all about?" He creased his tanned brow.

"Do you do a lot of cycling, Sir?"

"Oh, yes I do. I'm a member of a group. We go out all over the Downs at the weekends, brushes away the cobwebs, you know?"

Nate nodded. "Is there somewhere we could talk in private?"

Johnson looked cautious. He led them to a bench in the garden. He clearly sensed this might not be a conversation he'd want his wife to hear.

"We are investigating the suspicious death of a woman living in Hillingdon, south London. Her name was Autumn Carlisle."

A shadow passed across Johnson's features. "Holy shit."

"You remember her then?" Dani asked.

"*Of course*, I bloody do. She accused me of *rape*, for Christ's sake. I had to go to court and everything. But I was cleared. Thank God there were witnesses who could vouch for me." He glanced nervously at the house. "Elinor doesn't know anything about it."

"But the airline decided you'd been harassing Miss Carlisle during the outward flight. You were banned from flying with them."

Johnson balled his fists. "I was young and single. I'd had a few drinks before I got on the plane. I'd had a bad break-up back in London. I took that holiday to pull some birds, make me feel better. Autumn Carlisle was nice to me on the plane. I thought it was okay to flirt with her."

"The other passengers thought you were being a pest."

"Only later, when the police started asking questions and telling folk I'd been following her in Egypt and tried to attack her."

"Do you deny following Miss Carlisle to find out where she was staying?"

His mouth hardened in a grim line. "I took the tour bus to the resort at Sharm el Sheikh after the plane landed and stayed there, just like everybody else. I lay by the pool and drank myself stupid. I don't know who followed and attacked that woman, if anybody did, but it wasn't me."

Dani examined his face. Johnson's whole body was exuding anger and resentment. It was hard to recognise if he was telling the truth.

Elinor Johnson stepped out of the house and stood on the patio. "Is everything alright, Love?"

"Yeah, it's fine, Elinor. Go back inside."

Johnson lowered his voice. "Do you have to tell her anything?"

Nate shook his head. "Not if you co-operate. Had you seen Autumn Carlisle since the allegations made against you in 2011?"

He took a deep breath, as if trying to calm himself. "No, I had not. I never wanted to set eyes on her again." His face suddenly crumpled with incredulity. "You don't actually think I might have *killed* her, do you?"

"You certainly held a grudge against her," Dani said quietly.

"With good reason," he added through gritted teeth. "Look, whenever Autumn Carlisle kicked the bucket, I can provide you with chapter and verse on where I was. I usually work out of the office in Woking, but if I'm doing house visits for quotes, I've got GPS tracking in the company car. You can have the lot, an open book."

Nate scribbled the date of Autumn's death on a business card and handed it over. "These are my details. We'll be in touch in a few days."

The man got to his feet, examining the card closely. The detectives left through the side gate. Dani turned back as she climbed into the passenger seat. Johnson was still standing in the garden, glaring at them as they departed.

Nate shut the door and turned on the engine.

"I thought he reminded me of someone when we first arrived. Now I know who it is."

Nate raised his eyebrows inquisitively.

"John Lomond, Denny's brother. He watched us leave the house in Henley, much like Johnson is doing now. They're both dark haired, tall and with a similar build."

"I can see what you mean, but I'm sure it's just a coincidence." He reversed the Mercedes onto the empty road. "Now, what do you fancy for dinner?"

Chapter 23

Dermot Muir approached Sharon's workstation. He pulled up a chair to join her.

"I got a call from DCI Bevan a couple of days ago. She wanted me to run some checks for her, to assist with the case down in London."

Sharon eyed him carefully through her fringe of corkscrew curls. "How are they progressing down there?"

"A few leads have opened up, but it's a long slog, according to the DCI. The team need to scour through CCTV from all the cameras at Heathrow Terminal 1. You can imagine how many people appear in those images."

Sharon whistled. "I don't envy them that. Mind you, Andy and I had to sift through hours of extreme pornography for a previous case. That was worse, you could almost feel your soul being corrupted the more you watched."

"It got you a result, though."

Sharon nodded, impressed that Muir knew the case she was referring to. "Sometimes you just need to put in the hard graft."

"Speaking of which," Dermot flashed her a lopsided grin. "I wondered if you could help me out with this background check I've been running?"

Sharon leant back and folded her arms over her bosom. "Oh aye, let's hear the details."

"The parents of the first murder victim in the London investigation live in Cumbernauld. They are friends of Professor Morgan. Bevan wanted me to find out more about the mother; Betsy Carlisle. I've found out plenty about her husband, Mike, but I'm drawing a bit of a blank with her."

Sharon tapped on her keypad to fire up her screen. "Let's take a look. I'm assuming she will be an Elizabeth?"

Muir nodded. "That's what I thought. Her husband was born in '53. According to Morgan, Betsy is no more than a couple of years younger than him."

"What about a marriage certificate? That should provide you with a maiden name."

Dermot opened a file and pulled out the printout on top. "They married at Inverness Town Hall on the 21st August 1987. According to the certificate, Elizabeth Smith was 34 years old and Michael Francis Carlisle was 36." He shook the sheet in frustration. "I've checked the Scotland's People database for information about an Elizabeth Smith, born around 1955. There were dozens. I need more to go on if I'm going to pin her down properly."

"It's a very common surname. What about a birth certificate for the daughter?"

"Autumn was born on the 13th October 1988 at a private hospital, but her birth was also registered in Inverness."

Sharon drummed the keys of her computer for a couple of minutes. "Well, neither Elizabeth or Michael Carlisle show up on the Holmes database."

Dermot grimaced. "I didn't really expect them to. They are a very respectable couple, I don't imagine they've even got so much as a parking ticket between them."

Sharon twisted round to face her colleague. "You said there was more information available about the husband. What do you know about him?"

Dermot again referred to the documents in the

file which was balanced in his lap. "Michael Carlisle was born in Nairn. He has two brothers, one now deceased. His father was a schoolteacher and his mother a housewife. Michael studied modern languages at Aberdeen University. He then took a teaching qualification and was teaching and lecturing up to his retirement in 2012, including a stint in Inverness during the eighties."

"He must have met Elizabeth when he was working in the Inverness area." Sharon tucked a stray curl behind her ear. "They were both quite old when they married – by the standards of the time, I mean."

Dermot nodded. "Which suggests to me that they *both* had careers before tying the knot."

Sharon sighed. "The best way for you to find out about Betsy Carlisle's life is just to *ask* her, you know."

Dermot frowned. "Yes, I realise that. But Professor Morgan warned me off approaching her. Apparently, Mike feels his wife is in a very delicate state of mind right now. He doesn't even want Morgan to talk to her, let alone a detective inspector. Plus, I've got no jurisdiction to do so."

"Then Rhodri is going to have to give you more information to go on. He's known the family for decades, hasn't he? That's got to be your starting point. Unless you really want to track down every 'Smith' born in Scotland in the mid-fifties?"

Dermot certainly did not relish the idea of that. "You're right. I need to get back on to the Professor. Either he can tell me more, or he'll have to find a way of probing Mr and Mrs Carlisle further." He stood. "Thanks, Sharon. You've been a great help."

*

Professor Morgan had invited Dermot to his flat in

the north of the city. The DI had decided to call round on his way home from work.

Rhodri buzzed the entry door open and was waiting for his guest on the first landing. "DI Muir! Thank you for making the effort to visit my home. I didn't fancy all the rigmarole of coming to the station again. At least here, we can get a decent cup of coffee."

Dermot couldn't disagree with that logic. He followed the older man into a spacious, traditionally furnished flat. Rhodri led them straight to the pleasant lounge which boasted a high ceiling adorned with ornate cornices. A tray containing a cafetière of coffee lay on a table between two high-backed chairs.

"Please sit down." Rhodri took the seat which had a stack of papers balanced on the arm. "As you can see, I've been examining Betsy's medical notes thoroughly."

Dermot leant forward. "What were your conclusions?"

"Much as we discussed the other day. I would diagnose Betsy as suffering from a nervous disorder which at times can be serious and debilitating. If she were one of my patients; I would prescribe her a medium dose of a mood stabiliser and tell her to avoid highly stressful situations." Rhodri lifted the cafetière and proceeded to fill two cups. "Of course, the woman's daughter has just died – either by suicide or murder – so one can hardly make that suggestion in such circumstances."

Dermot left his coffee black and took a sip. "There were a number of entries which detailed Mrs Carlisle's dreams over a period of several months. What did you make of that?"

Rhodri furrowed his brow. "One of the practitioners the Carlisles approached to help Betsy was a specialist in *'the analysis of the subconscious'*, or so his website claims. He follows a Jungian practice of focussing on a patient's dreams. I don't subscribe to the technique myself, you understand."

"No, but the results seemed interesting?"

"Yes, particularly in the sense that Mike told Danielle and I that Autumn had been suffering from disturbing dreams in the months leading up to her death." Rhodri sipped thoughtfully from his cup. "According to those notes, Betsy also went through a phase of having nightmares, although it passed after a week or so."

"And those nightmares were about a plane crashing," Dermot went on. "I found the descriptions very vivid and disturbing. Wasn't her daughter an air-stewardess?"

"Yes, and the psychiatrist interpreted those dreams as a manifestation of Betsy's worries about the dangers of her daughter's job. She'd just started working for British Airways at the time. I must say, it's a convincing hypothesis."

"So, you don't think Betsy Carlisle was suffering from some kind of psychosis?"

Rhodri shook his head vigorously. "No, I see patients with her symptoms regularly. They are easy enough to keep under control."

Dermot drained his cup. "Then that is what I'll report back to DCI Bevan."

Rhodri edged forward in his seat. "What did you find out about the Carlisles when you performed the background check?"

Dermot ran a hand through his dark hair, which he would admit needed a trim. "Not a great deal, to be honest. Your friend Mike was a lecturer for his entire career. He came from the Nairn area and met Betsy when he was working in Inverness. Betsy, on the other hand, was harder to trace. She had a common maiden name in Scotland. I assume she was also working in the Inverness area when she met Mike."

"I suppose she must have been. Since I've known the couple, Betsy has always been at home; first with Autumn and then as a housewife to Mike. We've never spoken about any qualifications or training she might have had."

Dermot got to his feet. "Well, I don't think it's important now. The DCI was only really interested in Betsy's state of mental health and what bearing it had on her daughter. If you don't believe the woman is suffering from anything too serious, we can probably forget about her past, can't we?"

Rhodri remained seated, his thoughts were far away. "Yes, I expect you're right. Betsy can't possibly have anything to do with this unpleasant business."

Chapter 24

The Hammersmith Criminal Investigation Unit was full of officers squinting intently at computer screens. Dani weaved past the desks with a mug of tea in each hand. When she reached Lawrence's desk, she placed them down in any space she could find between sheets of paper.

"Cheers," Nate replied, without shifting his gaze from the digital recording playing out on his laptop.

Dani felt a pang of guilt. It was her suggestion to examine the CCTV for a suspect who might be dressed in a cleaner's overalls, but it seemed to be getting them nowhere.

Dani was cradling her cup as Trudy made her way towards them, an expectant expression on her face. "Sorry, I didn't think to make you one."

Trudy shook her head dismissively. "Not a problem, Ma'am." She held up her iPad, which was displaying a double-page spread from a newspaper. "I've found something interesting."

Nate finally looked up. "What is it, Trudy?"

The DC couldn't hide her excitement. "I know I'm supposed to be going through those CCTV tapes you emailed me, but I wanted to make sure I'd got all the information I could about the assault on Autumn in Egypt, so I spent the morning doing some digging."

Dani placed her tea on the desk, giving the detective her full attention.

"Reading through the police report made here in the UK, I picked up on a reference to the Egyptian investigation into Autumn's assault. Back when it happened in 2011, she hadn't reported the incident to the Egyptian police. But the British Authorities have good relations with Egypt, and they shared the information that Autumn gave them. The details were passed on to the police in Hurghada." Trudy pulled herself up a chair. "Now, my Arabic isn't up to much, but I called the Egyptian Embassy here in Mayfair. I thought someone might be able to get me a contact number in the Egyptian police force, preferably with an officer who spoke English."

"Good thinking." Dani was impressed.

"I spoke with one of the consular officials and he was extremely helpful. British tourism in Sharm el Sheikh is very important to the Egyptian economy. He recalled the case of Autumn Carlisle's attack very clearly."

"Did he?" Nate was taken aback. "It was nearly eight years ago!"

Trudy's tone became animated. "Yes, he remembered it because the case was only solved within the last few months."

Nate nearly choked on his mouthful of tea.

"The attack on Autumn matched the details of several reported sexual assaults on female tourists that had occurred in resorts along the Red Sea coast since 2008." Trudy enlarged the screen shot on her iPad and showed it to Nate. "The police had a rough description of the perpetrator – tall, muscular and with thick, dark hair. He was seen following young women before dragging them into undergrowth to assault them."

"Austin Johnson fits that description," Dani added.

"Yes, but the consulate official said he was quickly eliminated from their inquiries. Johnson wasn't in Egypt at the time of the other attacks."

"So, Johnson was definitely innocent," Nate commented evenly.

"The consulate emailed me this piece from a

British tourist magazine that is published in Cairo. It describes how the police in Hurghada finally tracked down the attacker. They had used DNA which was obtained from one of his rape victims to focus in on the perp. A man named Omar Salib, who worked at a car-hire desk at Sharm el Sheikh International airport was asked to provide a sample, along with his fellow male colleagues. He was a match. The case has been widely reported across the country. Salib stood trial in May and was convicted of multiple assault and rape offences."

Dani scanned the article. "Autumn can't have been asked to testify?"

"The consular official told me they used Autumn's police statement during the trial. She was informed of the man's arrest by the embassy. Her description of her attacker had been very thorough and provided an important part of the prosecution case. But they had enough evidence from his other victims, plus the DNA match, to convict him without her testimony. The police were overjoyed with this result. Alongside the fears of terrorist attacks, having a rapist on the loose was terrible for the tourist trade."

Nate pointed to an unfocussed photograph in the centre of the article, showing Salim being escorted into a court building. "He definitely resembles Austin Johnson in height and build."

Dani sighed. "I can see why she imagined it was him who attacked her. It seems Johnson was wrongly accused after all."

"Which doesn't mean to say he didn't still have a reason to hate Autumn," Nate put in.

"But his alibi for the night of Autumn's murder is pretty watertight," Trudy explained. "He was in the office in Woking during the day, but in the evening Johnson and his wife were out celebrating their anniversary. We've got witness statements from the restaurant they visited. The wife claims he was with her all night."

Dani handed the iPad back to Trudy. "I don't think we ever seriously saw him as a prime suspect in Autumn's murder, did we?"

Nate shook his head despondently. "No, we didn't. At least we have closure on the issue. I wouldn't have wanted to waste any more time on that line of enquiry."

Dani rested her hand on Trudy's shoulder. "That was excellent work. You can call Mr Johnson and tell him what you told us. I expect he'll be pleased that his name has been cleared. He should have been informed months ago, when the first arrest was made. I expect the news never got back to the officers who took Autumn's statement here in London."

Trudy smiled, pleased at being handed the responsibility. "I'll do that right now, Ma'am."

Chapter 25

Sharon Moffett was working late to complete some paperwork on a spate of gang-related acts of vandalism in Bridgton. She and Andy had been working on it since DCI Bevan's departure. Sharon had nearly finished when a flash in the corner of the screen indicated an email had landed in her inbox. It was from Stefan Bauer.

The DS immediately called up the message, intrigued by what the Bauers' older son might have to say. She quickly skimmed through the text.

Dear DS Moffett,
                 I am writing to thank you for your sensitive handling of my parents' unexpected deaths over in your city of Glasgow. The fact that they passed away in a foreign country made the whole situation more difficult for myself and my sister, Mila. I apologise if my tone was at times argumentative; this was because of the stress of the situation. Now I am back at home in Germany, I have been able to accept the situation better.

Klaus and Greta were laid to rest last Friday, at a cemetery in Wiesbaden. My parents were non-religious. The ceremony was a simple celebration of their lives. A pair of larch trees were planted in their honour. It may sound odd, but the passing of our mother and father together has come to provide Mila and I with some comfort. Neither would ever need to know the pain of losing the other.

Another comfort to us, was the letter we received from an old colleague of our father's. He had read of his death in the national press, where, due to his success in pharmaceutical research, Klaus had been given a brief obituary. He sent a letter via the drug company in Frankfurt where Dad spent the last years of his career. This man, Professor Fischer, remembered our father when they both worked in Berlin, over thirty years ago. Fischer is now suffering from early onset dementia, but he recalled working with Dad, as clearly as if it were yesterday. His letter provided us with more details about the projects Dad was involved in than he had ever divulged to me or Mila when he was alive. That part of his life had always been kept private. He described it as 'important government work'. We never dreamt to pry into it. They were hard times, when the Cold War was still at its height.

Anyway, I simply wanted to explain that the funeral has now taken place and to pass on the gratitude of our family for your hospitality when I came to Scotland. If you ever find yourself in Germany, Sergeant, we would hope to return the favour.

Best wishes,

Stefan Bauer

Frankfurt-am-Main

Sharon re-read the message a couple of times. She was relieved Stefan seemed to have made peace with his parents' deaths. There was always a risk that disgruntled relatives might continue to stir up trouble in a case as ambiguous as this one had been.

But quite the contrary, Stefan's tone was very conciliatory, although Sharon wasn't sure she'd done much to warrant his praise. In her opinion, the investigation proved unsatisfactory. The Fiscal's office was happy enough to rule the Bauers' deaths as due to natural causes, but the situation had still struck the DS as odd. Two unexplained deaths in the same place at the same time. Sharon didn't like coincidences.

The lights on the floor of the division were dimmed. She glanced in the direction of Bevan's office. It was dark inside and the door was closed. Sharon imagined DI Muir was long gone. She had to admit the man was efficient and amiable, but he wasn't one for burning the midnight oil.

She sighed, clicking the print button on the screen. She wanted to show Muir a copy of the message from Bauer first thing in the morning. Sharon had a feeling her new colleague would be interested in its contents.

*

Dani propped a couple of pillows behind her and made herself comfortable on the hotel's king-sized bed. She had a pad of paper and a complimentary pen in her hand. Dani proceeded to list the suspects in the murders of Autumn Carlisle and Kathy Brice.

She scored out the name of Austin Johnson, who seemed now to have been eliminated as a suspect due to his alibi on the night of Autumn's death. He appeared more like a victim himself, having been falsely accused of a terrible crime.

Kathy Brice's boyfriend, Tom Birch, was also out of the frame. A member of Nate's team had questioned Birch's work colleagues and obtained a time-coded credit card receipt for a bag of shopping from a Tesco Express in Farringdon which supported his claim he was nowhere near Heathrow when

Kathy was strangled.

This left Denny Lomond. He was a man who connected both of their victims. Dani thought about his younger brother, John. He'd been living with Denny at his property in Henley-on-Thames for the last couple of years. She reached for a cup of instant coffee which was placed on the bedside table, made using the dinky travel kettle on the refreshment tray. It tasted artificially creamy due to the synthetic milk she'd added to it from a tiny plastic dispenser.

The outline of John Lomond was imprinted upon her mind's eye, as he stood in the doorway to Denny's kitchen on that sunny afternoon. When she'd seen the silhouette of Austin Johnson in his garden in Woking, it had reminded her of this man.

John had appeared watchful of his brother on that day, protective, even. He had taken on the role of gardener since living at the house. The relationship between the two men appeared close, yet the younger had almost adopted for himself a subservient role: like an employee. Dani's mind kept ticking over, ruminating on their odd relationship as she sipped her drink.

When she got back to the criminal investigation department in the morning, the DCI was determined to look more closely into the backgrounds of Denny and John Lomond.

Chapter 26

Dermot had escorted Sharon out of the department, buying them both a coffee at a quiet café a few hundred yards along Pitt Street from the police headquarters.

"This is very kind of you, Boss," Sharon commented, as a tall latté was placed down in front of her.

"I didn't want the entire office speculating as to why we were talking so much." Dermot emptied a sachet of sugar into his own drink, which he was taking black.

"Calder, you mean?" Sharon chuckled. "He's already started calling me *teacher's pet*."

Muir rolled his eyes. "Not just Andy Calder. The DCS made it quite clear to me the Bauer case was closed. I'm not supposed to be doing anything during Bevan's absence other than keeping current live cases ticking over."

Sharon nodded. "Aye, well I've not told anyone else about the email from Stefan."

"Good. It will need to stay that way." Muir tipped his cup, taking a slug of his drink like it was a shot of the hard stuff. He felt the caffeine rush through his veins, jolting his nervous system awake. "I just can't help feeling we should have looked more closely at the background of the dead couple. I ran as many checks as I could from here, but I drew a blank on Bauer's professional life before re-unification in October 1990."

Sharon nodded. "But Stefan now has a letter giving him details of what his dad was up to during the Cold War. What we wouldn't give to take a read of that!"

Muir sighed. "We've got absolutely no jurisdiction to ask for a copy. The investigation into Klaus and Greta's deaths is well and truly closed. But I still feel a niggling doubt about it."

"Same here."

Muir rubbed his freshly shaved chin. "I expect the British intelligence service might be interested to get hold of that letter from Klaus's ex-colleague. They still have a file on him from when he was living in the GDR."

Sharon cradled her tall glass, half the contents already gone. "Would they really care now? The Cold War ended thirty years ago. The threat is from Islamic terrorism these days, isn't it?"

"Yes, primarily. But look at the cases of Novichok poisoning we've had on British soil in the last few years? These are, *allegedly,* examples of the FSB tracking down so-called traitors of the Cold War era. There are clearly plenty of people out there with very long memories."

"I suppose you're right. But if you pass the information onto the secret services and they contact Stefan Bauer, he's going to know I betrayed his confidence." She crinkled her brow. "I certainly don't think the Bauers were a threat to *British* security in any way."

"No, I agree. If Klaus's past was a threat to anybody, it was to him and his wife."

"What about Stefan and Mila – do you think they're safe?" Sharon was suddenly alarmed.

Muir shrugged, draining his cup. "If Stefan is being so open about the contents of that letter he received from Mr Fischer, I'd say maybe not."

"Bloody hell, I hadn't considered that."

"There's really not much we can do from here. I'll call my contact in Intelligence and pass on what we know. I don't expect he'll take any action on it. They're up to their eyes monitoring online activity between radical groups. This situation is hardly urgent. We've got no evidence anyone is in imminent danger."

Sharon leant back in her chair. "I know it's unlikely to serve any purpose, but I'd like to go back to the Berkley Hotel one more time, have a word with some of the domestic staff. Whilst there's still someone there who will recall the Bauers during their stay, I think it's worth having another shot."

Muir hunched his shoulders. "Take a couple of hours to head over there now. I'll cover for you with Calder. As long as DCS Douglas doesn't find out, I don't see the harm in it."

*

Sharon had slipped back into the department to scan the photograph of Klaus Bauer that was used to accompany his obituary in Die Welt. She stuffed the printout in her pocket before heading out again to the Trongate area of the city.

It was nearly lunchtime and the Berkley Hotel lobby was busy. It was clear that businessmen used the restaurant for working lunches. The dining room was full of dark suits, contrasted sharply against the cream leather chairs. The receptionists were busy with a large group who were checking in. Sharon edged past the throng and entered the lift, punching the button for the third floor.

The door to the room where the Bauers had been found dead was ajar. A cleaning trolley was parked in the corridor outside. A middle-aged black woman in a blue uniform emerged from another room, further along the corridor. She eyed Sharon suspiciously.

"Can I help you, Madam?"

Sharon held out her warrant card. "Have you worked here long?"

"Yes, for three years now." The cleaner had the faintest hint of a West Indian accent. "But I've lived in Glasgow all my life," she added in a defensive tone.

"Don't worry, I'm not from the immigration department." She dipped her head towards the half-open door. "Do you remember the couple who died in that room a couple of weeks ago – they were from Germany?"

She nodded. "Their English was very good. The man had a problem with his entry card when they first arrived. I went down to reception to fix it for them. He gave me a tip. I told him we don't accept cash from customers, but he should tell the manager he is pleased with my work."

Sharon pulled out the scanned image of Professor Bauer. "Was this the man?"

"Yes, he was always with his wife. They seemed a devoted couple."

Sharon cleared her throat. "Do you know who found them on the morning after they died?"

"It wasn't me, thank the Lord. It was Lysette. She had entered the room to clean, we have a key to them all. There wasn't any reply to her knock, so she thought the couple had gone down to breakfast."

"It must have been an awful shock. Is Lysette on duty now?"

"I think so. She's usually on the morning shift, like me. But I don't know which floor she'll be on. It's a big hotel. I only follow my own rota. We don't have time to socialise. The housekeeping office is beyond the reception desk, near the day spa."

"I'll find out for myself then. Thanks for your help."

Sharon decided to take the stairs back down to the lobby. Trolleys were stationed on each landing, transporting piles of clean towels and linen. It was a busy time of day for the hotel.

The door to the housekeeping office was shut. Sharon knocked briskly. An irritated voice demanded she enter. The room was windowless and cramped. A harassed looking man sat behind an untidy desk. A white board was hung on the wall behind him, bearing a rota of names and dates scrawled in marker pen. Sharon scanned it for the name, *Lysette*. But the handwriting was almost indecipherable.

"Can I help you?"

Sharon showed her ID. "I'm from the serious crime unit, Sir."

He shifted up higher in his seat.

"I was hoping to speak with an employee of yours by the name of Lysette? I was told she might be on duty this morning?"

The man shook his head. "You've been informed wrongly, I'm afraid. Lysette doesn't work here any longer. She moved to another hotel at the end of the month."

Sharon's heart sank. She didn't have the authority to go to another hotel and start asking questions. "But it *was* this, *Lysette*, who discovered the bodies of Mr and Mrs Bauer, the German couple who died, in their room?"

He nodded. "Yep, Mr Bartlett, the manager, gave her the rest of the day off. She came back for a few shifts after that, but the experience had really upset her."

"It's understandable."

"Then, out of the blue, she asks for a transfer, says she can't stay at the Berkley one minute longer. I wasn't happy, because she was a great worker." He grunted. "Which is difficult to find in this business, I can assure you."

"What do you mean by a transfer?" Sharon asked in bafflement.

"To another hotel in our chain." He summoned up a webpage and turned his computer monitor so she could read the logo running along the header in a cursive blue font. "Lysette Carson now works at The Triton out at Prestwick Airport. It was one of our very first establishments, which makes sense, what with our link to aviation."

Sharon blinked as she read the information on the screen. Something about the name of the hotel group was ringing a bell in her head. "So, the Berkley belongs to the Lomond group of hotels?"

"Aye, you've heard of Lomond Airlines, right?"

"Sure, the CEO is Scotland's answer to Richard Branson!"

"Well, he's our big boss. I think Denny Lomond opened the hotel at Prestwick before he ever started up the airline business. Nowadays, it feels like we're a bit of an afterthought in the Lomond empire. He's closed several of his hotels over the past decade. All that remains are The Berkley, The Triton, and The Highlander, up near Inverness."

Sharon absorbed this information in silence.

"So, I can't really help you any further, Detective. But you can have a card for The Triton. I'll write the name of the Domestic Services Manager there on the back, if you like?"

Sharon forced herself to focus on what the man was saying. "Yes, please. That would be great."

Chapter 27

It was difficult for Dani to find a free computer. In the end, she used her own iPad, finding a space on an old battered sofa by the water dispenser to position herself. The rest of the team were still busy examining the CCTV footage.

The DCI already knew that Denny Lomond was free from criminal convictions. They had run checks on all the suspects in the two murder cases. His full name was Dennis Karl Lomond. Through an internet search, Dani had found an interview with the entrepreneur which had featured in The Scotsman in 2016. It was a lengthy piece in a weekend supplement. She decided to start with that.

The interview was focussing on Lomond's decision to begin operating his low-budget airline out of Heathrow. Lomond mentioned his wife's tragic death from lung cancer, at the age of just 34, as the motivating factor. He had no reason to be tied to Scotland any longer. It was time to expand the business and devote himself body and soul to his work.

Dani was intrigued to discover Denny had begun his career in the hotel business. He joined a catering college straight from school and began working for one of the big hotels in Glasgow. Denny used hard graft and initiative to work his way up to becoming manager.

The young businessman then noticed an advert in a national paper. A large old country house was up for sale near where he grew up. It was in desperate need of repair and going relatively cheap. Denny visited his bank manager and begged for them to give him a mortgage on the property, despite its dilapidated state. His persistence made the bank take a chance on him.

Denny continued in his day job, spending every moment of his free time renovating the old house. Finally, after two years of hard labour, the country house was ready to open as a hotel. It was the first in a chain that was to end up servicing every major town and city in Scotland.

Dani leaned across to pour herself a cup of water. Denny was clearly a very determined and ambitious man. To build up a business empire from nothing was no mean feat. She scrolled further down the page. Once Denny's chain of hotels was established and the money coming in, he turned his attention to his real love – aeroplanes.

Lomond already had a thriving hotel at Prestwick Airport, but now he had the capital, the entrepreneur began to build up a fleet of aircraft.

Dani skimmed through the remainder of the article. It chronicled the highs and lows of the early days of Lomond Airlines. How Denny mortgaged his hotels to the hilt in order to launch the airline business, a major gamble when so many other small British airlines had gone to the wall. But this was Denny's dream, he was prepared to risk everything.

It was during the early years of Lomond Airlines, that Denny met a young Kelly Boyd. She was an airhostess on one of the company's first flights out of Prestwick. They fell in love and married within a year. Dani sipped her water. The story of how Kelly discovered she was suffering from stage four lung cancer was heart-breaking.

There was a photograph of the young woman, cradled in Denny's arms. She was clearly still beautiful, but the disease had made her skin pallid and her body skeletal.

Dani wasn't surprised Denny decided to leave Scotland not long after his wife's death. It must have been painful for him to remain in the place where they'd been so happy. The decision to set himself up in a large airport like Heathrow – sprawling and anonymous, must have felt like a fresh start.

Information about Denny's brother, John, wasn't so easy to come by. It always amazed Dani that in this modern, digital age, some people's entire lives were an open book. All you needed to do was tap into a few search engines and an individual's often intimate details and experiences were laid bare for all to see. Yet others could remain completely anonymous. John Lomond was an example of the latter. His name was relatively common and his life unremarkable. Dani knew she'd have to use the police databases and online birth and marriage registries to find out anything at all about the younger Lomond brother.

As Dani stretched her back, which was suffering after even a brief stint on the badly sprung sofa, Nate approached her along the corridor.

"So, *this* is where you've been hiding." He accompanied the words with a grin.

She held up her hands. "Guilty as charged."

Nate cocked his head. "We may have just found something interesting at last."

Dani sprung to her feet. "Great, show me what you've got."

The image was grainy. It showed a tall man in the Lomond Airways cleaners' uniform pushing a trolley towards one of the passport control areas at Heathrow. The time code indicated it was 5.24pm on the afternoon of Kathy Brice's murder.

"I know the picture isn't very clear," Nate said apologetically, "but I'm hoping the techies can clean it up for us."

Trudy tapped the screen. "The DC who was examining this piece of footage also had a list of all the domestic employees who were on shift at Lomond during the time period in question. The only cleaning staff authorised to be working at the airport were female."

Dani squinted at the blurred figure in the shot. "And this is definitely a man."

"Precisely," Nate added.

"Where is he headed to?"

Trudy pointed to the passport control desk visible on the frozen image. "Beyond that desk is a corridor with access to gates 50-60."

Dani clapped her hands. "Kathy was killed at gate 52."

"Bingo," said Nate. "But we shouldn't get too excited. All we have is a fuzzy profile of a man. The techies will be able to ascertain his height. His hair appears to be a sandy blond. But he could easily be wearing a wig. I certainly would if I was about to commit a murder in an area dotted with cameras."

Dani sighed. "You're right." She laid a hand on his shoulder. "But we've now got a picture of a man who must surely be the prime suspect for Kathy's killer. He had to be a person who would have access to a Lomond Airlines uniform and security pass. That gives us something solid to work on."

Nate straightened himself up to his full height. "We need to make another visit to Lomond Airlines. This time around, we won't let ourselves be fobbed off."

Chapter 28

The second Andy Calder grabbed his jacket from the back of his chair and told his colleague he was off home, Sharon hurried towards Bevan's office. She could see that Muir was still in there, leaning over the desk. He glanced up as Sharon drummed her knuckles on the flimsy window.

"Any luck at the hotel?" He asked with genuine interest.

Sharon closed the door firmly behind her and took a seat. "I found out the member of the domestic staff who discovered the Bauers dead was a woman called Lysette Carson. She's 44 years old and lives in Govan with her husband and kids."

"Did you interview her?"

Sharon shook her head. "At the time of the Bauers' deaths, the hotel manager told me the cleaner who found them was sent home on compassionate leave, which was fair enough. He also assured me the room had been left exactly as she'd found it. We weren't treating the deaths as suspicious, so I took the man at his word."

"Do you have reason to doubt him now?"

"I'm not sure. Lysette came back to the Berkley for a few days and then demanded to be re-located to another hotel in the chain. She's now working at the Triton at Prestwick."

"Damn. It's going to be tricky to question her there. The manager may want to speak with the DCS, to check our jurisdiction."

Sharon ran a hand through her unruly curls. "Don't you find it odd that Lysette left the hotel so swiftly?"

"Well, if I'd seen two corpses at my place of work, I might have second thoughts about staying there myself."

"Yeah, I get that. But they'd only died in their sleep. I saw the scene myself. They looked pretty peaceful." Sharon summoned a map of the city onto her phone screen. "Look, the Berkley was a lot more convenient for Lysette to get to than Prestwick Airport. She's got a hell of a commute now."

"You think it may not have been her decision to leave?"

Sharon nodded. "That's exactly what I think. I did some checking on the system. Lysette moved to Scotland from Srebrenica in the late nineties. She married a Scot and settled here. I expect she's seen far worse in her life than an elderly couple who died apparently peacefully in their sleep."

Muir considered this. "You're right. Something about it doesn't add up."

Sharon leaned in closer. "There's something else. The Berkley is part of a chain of hotels. I hadn't realised that before. The hotels are owned by Denny Lomond – you know, the aeroplane guy? That struck me as significant, but I'm not sure why."

Muir gave a start. "It's DCI Bevan's case down in London. The victim was a stewardess for Lomond Airlines. Bevan told me they've been questioning Denny Lomond as a potential suspect."

Sharon's eyes widened. "That's it! I read about the woman's death on the BBC news site. I took an interest because I knew the boss was involved. It mentioned the victim worked for Lomond, but I didn't take much interest at the time."

Muir glanced at his watch. "Should we bother the DCI with this? It's just a coincidence that doesn't really have any bearing on her case?"

Sharon let out a snort of derision. "If DCI Bevan

discovers we knew this fact and didn't tell her, our lives will not be worth living in this place when she gets back."

Muir didn't hesitate any further. He got out his phone, scrolling through the contacts until he found Bevan's number.

*

This time the detectives entered the office of Denny Lomond's secretary, they were holding a warrant from a judge at West London Magistrates' Court.

Diane Martin abruptly ended a conversation she was having on the phone. "I'm afraid you didn't call ahead to warn me. Mr Lomond is very busy. All day."

Nate placed the official document on the desk in front of her. "We have been authorised to search these premises. Please inform Mr Lomond that we wish to talk to him. If he can't do it here, we will have to arrest him and do it at the Hammersmith police station."

A figure appeared in the doorway beyond. "There's no need for that, Detective Inspector. Come into my office. I'm sure we can co-operate reasonably with your demands."

Denny Lomond disappeared inside. The detectives followed. There was no offer of refreshments on this occasion.

All three remained standing.

Nate showed the CEO a copy of the still from the CCTV footage. "This man, caught on camera wearing a Lomond Airline's uniform was heading towards the gate where Kathy Brice was murdered, just minutes before her death."

"Your Domestic Services Manager furnished us with a list of personnel on duty that afternoon. Not one of them was a man," Dani added.

"We need to identify this person urgently, Mr

Lomond. Do you recognise him?"

He peered at the image, slowly shaking his head. "I've never seen that person before. Although, it isn't a very clear picture, is it? Surely it wouldn't be of any use in a court of law?"

Nate could feel his anger bubbling up. "How many men do you have working for you as cleaners, Sir?"

"A few. You'll have to get their details from the Domestic Manager. He'll be happy to help." Lomond's expression was impassive, he was giving nothing away.

"Doesn't it concern you that Kathy Brice may very well have been murdered by a man who had access to a Lomond Airlines' uniform? He must also have had one of your security passes in order to have got past passport control."

Denny shrugged. "It's unfortunate, but I'm sure it can't have been one of my staff. We have them all very closely vetted."

Dani decided to change tack. "Yes, but isn't it also *unfortunate* that a couple were found dead at one of your hotels in Glasgow a fortnight ago?"

The man's eyes displayed a tiny flicker of concern. It was gone in an instant, but both detectives had seen it. He hadn't been expecting that question.

"I've spoken at length with the manager of the Berkley about that tragic incident. But the Fiscal's findings were conclusive; the couple were elderly, both suffered from pre-existing heart conditions. Their deaths were due to natural causes. A tragedy for their family back home in Germany, I'm sure." Denny stood still with his legs slightly apart, the pose was almost combative.

Dani sighed deeply, theatrically. "Tragedy just seems to follow you around, doesn't it, Mr Lomond?"

The man took a step forward, his hands forming into fists. "What do you mean by that *exactly*?" He growled.

Nate put an arm out to shield his colleague. "Whoa there, lets calm it down a little, shall we?"

"I meant, first Autumn Carlisle's bloody death, then Kathy Brice is brutally murdered whilst working out of this building and then two bodies wind up in what turns out to be another of your commercial premises." Dani looked him straight in the eye. "Why? What did *you* think I meant?"

Lomond curled his lip into what could only be described as a snarl.

"Right. I suggest we go and get the information we need from the Domestic Services Department," Nate declared. "Don't leave the building, Mr Lomond. We may be required to speak with you again before we return to the station."

Nate hustled Dani out into the corridor. "What the hell was that all about?"

Dani shuddered. "I think we've just caught a glimpse of the real Denny Lomond, and it wasn't pleasant."

Chapter 29

Dermot and Sharon approached the block of flats together. There was no buzzer to gain entry to the communal staircase. The grey concrete walls emitted the aroma of stale urine, as if it had seeped into the very core of the building.

The Carson family resided on the second floor. The door to their flat was accessed along an open balcony, with views over the sprawling south Glasgow estate.

Sharon pressed the bell. She could see a flash of movement within. It took a few moments before a thin woman answered. Lysette Carson was wearing a grey tracksuit with pink piping, her hair pulled back into a pony-tail.

"Mrs Carson? We're from the Serious Crime Unit. May we come in?" Sharon made sure the woman examined her ID carefully.

Lysette retreated into the flat. She stopped in the living room, which was sparsely furnished but neat and tidy. "What is this about?" Her voice was wary.

"It's nothing to worry about, purely routine." Sharon perched on the arm of a sofa. "I was supposed to interview you a couple of weeks ago, back when you were working at the Berkley hotel. But you were off sick. Then I found out you'd changed jobs. So, I've come to talk to you here, instead."

"Is this about the couple who died?"

"Yes," Dermot added. "You were the person who found them, weren't you?"

She nodded. "I was on duty on their corridor that morning. It was my job to clean all the rooms. It had to be done by 11.30am. There is always pressure."

"I can imagine," Sharon said gently. "Could you talk us through what happened on that particular day?"

Lysette inched towards the window, as if searching for a means of escape. "Mr Bartlett told me not to talk to the police."

"The manager of the Berkley Hotel?" Sharon became alert.

Dermot raised his eyebrows. "Why on earth did he say that?"

Lysette shrugged. "He wanted to handle the situation himself. He said it was *damage limitation.* The deaths were bad publicity for the hotel. He would handle any interviews."

"It was part of a police investigation," Dermot said levelly. "*We* decide who to interview."

She nodded her head. "I know that. But Mr Bartlett was my boss, I had to do what he said. After a few days, he told me I must move to the hotel at Prestwick. I tried to complain but he said I must go, they were understaffed at the Triton, desperate for cleaners."

"Why do *you* think he made you transfer to another hotel?" Sharon kept her tone kindly.

"I heard the children of the German couple were coming to look at where their parents died. Within a few hours of this news, I was told I needed to go." She flicked her pony-tail in a defiant gesture. "I believe Mr Bartlett wanted me out of the way, in case these people tried to speak to me about what I saw."

Sharon sucked in her breath. "Will you tell us what you saw?"

"I don't want to lose my job."

"Mr Bartlett isn't your boss any more. What can he do?"

She shrugged. "I have been thinking this myself. I

am doing a very good job at the Triton. The manager is a lady and she is pleased with my work. I think she would object to anyone sacking me. Besides, this is Scotland. You can't sack a person for no good reason. I'm not some frightened illegal immigrant who can be bullied and intimidated. I am a British citizen."

"Quite right, Mrs Carson." Dermot puffed out his chest. "If you talk to us, we give you our reassurances that your job will be safe."

Lysette cast him a doubtful glance but proceeded to speak anyway. "I had completed a quarter of the bedrooms on my corridor. When I reached the room of the German couple, there was no reply to my knock. It was after 9am, this usually means the occupants are at breakfast. This couple were early risers. So, I opened the door with my key card." She took a deep breath. "The man and lady were stretched out on the bed, neither of them moving."

"On top of the covers?" Sharon tried not to sound surprised.

She nodded. "They were in their night clothes. The lady was curled up like a baby, her hands at her throat and the man was clutching his chest." She sighed. "Sadly, I have seen many dead bodies before. I grew up in Bosnia during the war. I saw the bodies of my father and brothers in a pit. I looked at the expressions on their faces. I wanted to know how they had felt, to understand what they went through in those last moments. I saw something similar on the faces of that couple."

Sharon gasped. When she'd seen the Bauers, they were tucked up under the covers, their expressions the picture of serenity.

"It was terror that I saw. There were no signs of violence on their bodies, not like the bullet wounds in my father and brothers. But their faces told their own stories. The couple had been frightened to death."

Dermot asked softly, "what did you do after finding the bodies?"

"I went downstairs to tell the Domestic Services Manager. He is a decent man, he sent me home for the day, said I would be in shock. He made sure I got paid for a full shift."

"You never went back up to the bedroom?"

"No, I had no reason to. I knew the manager would call the police. I expected to be questioned at some point, but it never happened. Then, Mr Bartlett told me I would be changing hotels and that I should keep my mouth shut."

Sharon got to her feet. "Would you be prepared to give us a signed statement setting out exactly what you've just said?"

"Why not. It is the truth, after all."

Dermot stepped forward and shook her hand. "Thank you, Mrs Carson. I wish you and your family all the best in the future."

Chapter 30

The dawn was starting to break as Rhodri Morgan drove along the M80 towards Cumbernauld. He had received a phone call from Mike Carlisle in the early hours. The man was frantic, worried his wife was having some form of psychotic episode.

Rhodri had calmed his friend down as best he could, entreating him to make sure Betsy was safe until he got there.

The professor had left early enough to ensure the motorway was clear of traffic. He reached the Carlisle's stone property by breakfast time. One of the neighbours was emerging from the house next-door in a smart suit, unlocking an executive car on the driveway.

Mike opened the door as Rhodri approached. He'd clearly been watching for his arrival. The man had dressed in a rush; the collar of his shirt turned up and his grey hair ruffled at the temples.

"Rhodri, thank you so much for coming. I wasn't sure what to do."

Rhodri put down his briefcase in the hall. He noticed Dodie curled up in a basket in the kitchen, her jet-black eyes held his; they were full of sadness. This wasn't the excitable pup he'd encountered on his last visit. The dog had obviously picked up on the fraught atmosphere in the house, the odd behaviour of its owner.

As he drew closer, Rhodri saw that Betsy was pacing the length of the sitting room, still in her dressing gown. Mike was propped on the arm of one of the chairs, looking on helplessly.

Rhodri moved closer to her. "Betsy," he said

softly. "It's Rhodri here. I've come to see if I can help. Won't you sit down?"

Betsy fixed him with a curious stare, as if she'd never set eyes on him before. She continued to march up and down, like a soldier on parade. The professor noticed then that she was muttering under her breath. He laid a hand on her shoulder. She stopped dead in her tracks.

Rhodri led her very gently by the arm to the sofa, guiding her onto the seat cushion. "Could you brew some tea, Mike? Make it nice and sweet."

Betsy's taut body seemed to relax just a fraction.

Rhodri positioned himself on a tasselled footstool in front of her. "It's Professor Morgan, Betsy. Do you know who I am?"

She nodded almost imperceptibly. The muttering continued.

"That's good. I'm here to help. I know it's been a difficult time for you. But this difficulty will pass. Things will get easier, I promise."

Betsy glanced up, her mutterings becoming louder, more audible. "We watched from the window. They tried to pull him out, but the flames were too high. He wasn't dead yet, you see. I saw his face – the absolute terror in his eyes."

Mike came in with a tray of teas. He set one down on the table beside his wife. "She's been saying the same thing since waking up in the middle of the night. I expect it was triggered by a bad dream."

"Has she taken her pills?"

Mike shook his head, "I don't think so, not in all the panic."

"That's fine, but go and fetch them now, will you?" Rhodri made sure the tea was cool enough to drink before placing the cup in Betsy's hands. "Take a sip."

She obediently put the cup to her lips,

spluttering on a mouthful, but gulping some down. When Mike returned with a glass of water and a couple of white pills, they did the same.

"It will help to calm her down," Rhodri whispered to his friend. "She should feel the effects in a little while."

Betsy slumped back against the cushions, as if utterly exhausted. "The beautiful trees were scorched. A gap had formed in the forest where there hadn't been one before. Those lovely red maple leaves. It's why I gave her that name, Autumn. Her hair was the colour of maple syrup."

Mike sat beside his wife, holding her hand. "Shush now, dear. It was so long ago, there's no need to dwell."

She twisted her head sharply. "They buried the body – not that there was much left of it. But what about a funeral? His family would have needed to say goodbye. It wasn't right."

Mike rubbed her hand. "It was all so long ago, don't let it upset you."

"I want to go back there. I want to go to Balloch House. I felt safe there. *Please*, Mike." Betsy gripped her husband's hand and her eyes searched his. "I want to go back there to die."

Mike gasped. "You're not going to die, darling."

Betsy's body slackened and her eyes closed.

"Let her rest," Rhodri whispered to his friend.

The two men carried their mugs into the kitchen. Mike perched on a stool at the breakfast bar. His pale face was pinched with worry. "What should I do?"

"She will most likely sleep for a few hours now. You need to contact the local mental health team. I'll find the appropriate numbers for you. They will come out and assess her."

"Will they take her away?" His expression was

panicked.

"They may decide she needs to be hospitalised for a few days, perhaps given sedation to help her through this difficult patch." He sighed. "You've both been through a terrible ordeal. Losing a child in such shocking circumstances is bound to have an impact." He patted his friend on the arm. "Betsy will get better."

"Sometimes I think that will never happen."

Rhodri narrowed his eyes. "What was she talking about earlier? Her ramblings seemed to focus on a person trapped in a fire. Is this something Betsy actually witnessed?"

Mike shrugged, his eyes fixed on the middle distance. "She's been ranting about it ever since waking in the night. I think it was the subject of her nightmare. She's certainly never mentioned it before."

"And what about Balloch House? Is it a place where you used to live?"

Mike sipped his tea. "It's a property near Inverness. We visited there once, that's all. She doesn't know what she's saying."

Rhodri didn't probe any further, he could see Mike was washed out himself. "You should go and lie down too. Whilst Betsy rests, it's an opportunity for you to get some sleep. You need to maintain your own health in order to see your wife through these next few days."

Mike nodded wearily. "You're right. But I need to take Dodie for a walk first. The poor thing's been waiting for hours."

"I'll take her," Rhodri surprised himself by saying. "You just get yourself upstairs."

Mike did as he was told, shuffling out of the kitchen door like a Zombie.

Rhodri found the dog's lead on a hook by the

back door, along with a house key. "Right," he said purposefully to Dodie's doleful, upturned face. "Let's get some fresh air, shall we?"

Her tail immediately began to wag.

Chapter 31

On this visit to the Berkley Hotel, with DI Muir in tow, Sharon was determined to make her presence felt. After his phone conversation with DCI Bevan and the information they'd gained from Lysette Carson, Muir had secured the permission of DCS Douglas to re-interview the hotel's manager.

It was a quieter time of day. The lobby was nearly empty. Sharon marched straight along the corridor where she knew Mr Bartlett's office was situated. She gave the door a perfunctory knock before entering. Muir followed.

Bartlett got immediately to his feet. It took him a few moments to recognise the detective, but when he did, his expression formed into a tight smile that did not reach his eyes.

"Detective Sergeant Moffett. I didn't expect to see you back here."

"No, I imagine not. This is Detective Inspector Muir. We need to ask a few more questions about the deaths of Mr and Mrs Bauer."

The man swept out from beside his desk and gestured for them to sit down on the plush sofa that lined the darkly panelled wall. "Certainly, but please make yourselves comfortable first."

"We're comfortable standing, thank you." Muir stayed where he was.

Sharon made a point of carefully reading through the last two pages of her notebook. "We had a very enlightening conversation with Mrs Lysette Carson, yesterday."

Bartlett's face paled. "Lysette doesn't work at this hotel any longer."

"No, but she did work here a couple of weeks ago. In fact, she was the person who discovered the bodies of Mr and Mrs Bauer."

"Yes, that's correct. The experience was very traumatic for the poor woman. She requested a move to another of our hotels. I hear she's doing very well there." He brushed non-existent fluff from his lapels.

"Except, that isn't what she told us. According to Mrs Carson, it was *you* who made her transfer to another place of work. She says you warned her not to speak to the police about what she saw that morning." Sharon tipped her head to one side, eyeing him quizzically.

He chuckled nervously. "That's not quite how I remember it. I simply wanted to handle the police enquiries myself. The incident could have been a marketing disaster for the hotel. Mr Lomond instructed me to handle the police personally."

"So, Mr Lomond was involved in the decision to move Mrs Carson to another hotel? Did he come here to Glasgow?"

Bartlett shook his head. "It was all done over the phone. Mr Lomond was at home in London."

Sharon took a step forward. She recited Lysette's description of how she found the Bauers' bodies the morning after their deaths. The detective paused to allow the words to sink in. "But when the police and pathologist arrived later that day, we saw quite a different scene. The Bauers were lying peacefully under the covers, the room pristine. How do you explain the discrepancy, Sir?"

Bartlett dropped down onto the sofa and placed his head in his hands. "I panicked," he muttered.

"I beg your pardon?" Muir added impatiently.

The man looked up. "When I saw the state of the German couple, I knew there would be problems for us. The publicity would be awful. I sent Lysette home and made sure myself and Rob were the only ones who had seen the room as it was."

"Rob is the manager of Housekeeping?"

He nodded. "I called Mr Lomond on my mobile phone. I explained what had happened. He told me exactly what to do. Rob and I moved the bodies." He licked his lips; his skin had turned a greenish tint. "Their positions hadn't yet become rigid. We were able to manoeuvre them under the covers. It was even possible to relax the muscles in their faces and close their eyes."

Sharon shook her head in exasperation. "You must have known that what you were doing was terribly wrong?"

He caught her gaze, his eyes entreating. "This is my job, my livelihood. I've got a wife and children to support. I'd been given an order from my superior."

"The Bauers had children too. They deserve to know what really happened to their parents." Muir's tone was frosty.

"Was there any sign of forced entry into the room?" Sharon was determined to regain some control over the investigation.

"No, Lysette had used her key to enter the room when there was no response from inside."

"Did you remove anything from the room when you tampered with the bodies?"

He shook his head vigorously. "We only moved the bodies, I swear. Just to make their deaths look," he paused. "More natural."

Sharon grunted. "But what you saw wasn't *natural,* was it? Lysette said the poor couple looked like they'd been utterly terrified, like something or someone had hounded them to their deaths. Did you think the same? Is that why you interfered with the scene?"

Bartlett's eyes darted about the office. "I need to

call a lawyer. I don't want to say any more."

"Fine," Muir took a step forward. "You can call your legal representative from the station. Charles Bartlett, I'm arresting you on suspicion of attempting to pervert the course of justice as set out in the criminal justice and licensing bill. You do not have to say anything, but I should warn you that it may harm your defence if you do not mention when questioned anything which you may later rely on in court."

Bartlett looked shell-shocked. "What about Rob? And Mr Lomond?"

"Oh, don't worry. We'll be arresting them too."

Chapter 32

Dani let her fist drop down on the desk in frustration. "DI Muir has just sent me the records from the hotel manager's mobile phone network."

"Oh yes?" Nate glanced up with interest.

"Bartlett made a twenty-minute call to the landline in Denny Lomond's office at quarter past nine on the morning the Bauer couple were found dead at the Berkley."

"That's good news, isn't it?"

"It backs up Bartlett's claim Lomond put him up to cleaning up the death scene, but we've got no transcript of the conversation. Lomond's lawyer is just going to deny that Denny gave the order for the bodies to be moved. It's his word against the hotel manager. The head of housekeeping got his orders from Bartlett. He didn't even know Denny had been involved. We've not got enough to arrest him for this. That bastard is just too slippery." Dani tipped her head back and looked up at the ceiling, letting her breath out in a long, slow puff.

"We don't simply want to nail Lomond on an attempt to pervert the course of justice charge, do we?" Nate's tone was serious. "We've now got the man connected to *four* suspicious deaths. I'd rather we found out if Lomond had any link to this German couple. What if he wasn't only concerned about the reputation of his hotel? What if he actually played a part in their deaths?"

Dani snapped her head back down to face her colleague. "But we know Lomond was definitely in London on the night the Bauers died."

"We also know Lomond has an alibi for the time

when Kathy Brice was strangled and for the night Autumn Carlisle's wrists were slit. It doesn't mean he wasn't involved. I don't get the feeling Lomond is a man who cleans his own dirty laundry, if you know what I mean."

Dani did know. She thought of John Lomond, busy at work in Denny's garden, acting like an employee rather than a family member; watchful and protective. "What about the brother? Do we know where he was at the times of the murders?"

Nate furrowed his brow. "We've got no grounds to question him. The man has no connection to the victims that we know of. I can try and find out, but Lomond's lawyers aren't going to like it if they get wind."

Dani considered this for a moment. "John Lomond has been down in London for three years, right? Denny said he's been living at the house all that time. It seems like he helps out around the place, but what about a job? Surely a fit bloke like him must have wanted to earn his own money during that time?"

Nate nodded slowly. "I'll check it out."

"While you do that, I'll get Dermot and Sharon to send me over everything they already know about Klaus and Greta Bauer. If there's any kind of connection between that couple and Denny Lomond, by God, I'm going to damn well find it."

*

Rhodri was back at his flat in Glasgow. The sky had turned dark outside the tall windows of his sitting room. The trees and twisting paths of Kelvingrove Park laid out below looked sinister in the gloom. The professor decided to lower the blinds.

He poured a glass of whisky from a bottle on the

sideboard, lifted his mobile phone and dialled.

"Rhodri?" A faint voice spoke on the other end of the line.

"Hello, Mike. I called to see how Betsy was." He took a gulp of whisky, feeling it warm his gullet on the way down.

"The doctor came over not long after you left. Betsy was talking nonsense again. He gave her a sedative and asked me to drive her to the clinic. They're going to keep her there until the weekend. She needs absolute rest."

"If that's what the professionals think, then it will be for the best. They will look after her, Mike." Rhodri was disappointed, he'd hoped after taking her medication and getting some rest, Betsy would have been more lucid. He'd had to leave before she woke. She was out for the count after her unsettled night.

For a typical psychotic attack, her behaviour had not been extreme; there were no violent outbursts and acts of self-harm. She had appeared in a trance-like state, certainly, but at no point did Betsy pose a threat to herself or others. The professor was surprised they'd taken her in, especially with pressure for beds being as it was.

"Yes, I'm sure they will. They left me some leaflets about dealing with grief. There are a few numbers to call for support. I might ring them in the morning."

"I think that's a great idea. There may even be a support group in your area. I'll check it out online for you. By the way, what's the name of your consultant, I might know him?"

"Dr Acharya. His clinic is in Kilsyth; it's part of the East Dunbartonshire Trust. He was very understanding and patient, even though Betsy was being rather difficult."

"He will be used to far worse cases than Betsy's, I can assure you. I've not heard of him, but I'm certain he's good."

"Thank you for your help, Rhodri. I'm not sure what I would have done without you, I didn't know where else to turn."

"Not at all, Mike. Now, make sure you use these few days to get plenty of sleep yourself. That's doctor's orders!"

Mike managed a chuckle. "I will do that. The last twenty-four hours has tired me to the bone."

After he ended the call, Rhodri felt exhausted himself. It was understandable, he decided, having made a round trip to Cumbernauld and walked for what felt like miles with an overly energetic puppy tugging him along the whole way. The professor smiled. He'd actually quite enjoyed it. The dog reminded him of when his boys were young. They took their yellow Labrador for long walks over the fields behind their house. Times that would never return.

He finished his whisky, determined not to become maudlin. But the words that had spilled out of Betsy's mouth whilst she was having her psychotic episode kept swirling around in his head. The incident involving a man trapped in a wreckage, left to burn alive. Somebody burying his body without informing the relatives. Mike dismissed these words as nonsense, but hadn't he also told her to try and forget – that it was all in the past? *What* was it that was all in the past, he wondered?

Had the events she described been a memory rather than a dream? Rhodri thought back to the psychiatric reports he and DI Muir had read. They referred to a spate of bad dreams about a plane wreck. Was this the same event Betsy was recalling that very morning?

The professor felt a dull ache tighten across his temples. He needed to sleep. Tomorrow, he would consider Betsy's words further.

Chapter 33

Arthur Keating's painting was still propped up against the mirror on the dressing table. Dani examined it for a while. The colours were muted to the point of being almost monochrome. She supposed this was intended to show the effect of the blackened wreckage of the plane on the surrounding vegetation.

The only hint of colour was evident in the auburns and browns of the leaves which still clung to the tallest branches of the trees. The crash must have occurred in Autumn, Dani surmised. The DCI was abruptly reminded of the maple trees which overlooked Autumn's cottage in Mitchling; the ones she had coveted but the new owner despised.

Dani wondered why Autumn had felt such a fascination for those trees, which blotted out the natural light to her garden and for this painting, which was deeply disturbing in its subject matter.

A laptop lay open on the bed. Dani pulled it onto her lap in order to continue her research. She'd decided the key to Denny's character lay in his professional life. There was no record of where he or his brother went to school, but Dani discovered Denny had achieved a City and Guilds qualification in hospitality from the College of West Scotland in Paisley when he was 19 years old. This gained him his first job in a hotel in Glasgow.

During this time, Klaus and Greta Bauer were living in Frankfurt with their children, Stefan and Mila. Dani couldn't identify a way in which the lives of these people could have crossed over with Lomond's. Dani was shaking her head in frustration when her mobile phone buzzed beside her on the duvet. She picked it up.

"Bevan here."

"Good evening, Ma'am. I hope it's okay to call you this late?"

"Hi Sharon, it's fine. I'm still working. Have you got something?"

"I emailed Stefan back, like you suggested. I didn't tell him we've re-opened the case just yet, but I said we were tying up a few loose ends. I asked why his parents had stayed at the Berkley Hotel in particular, and if they'd ever used the hotel before?"

"Has he replied?"

"Yes, I just got the message a few minutes ago. He says it was a new destination for his parents. According to Stefan, his mum won one of those online competitions. The prize was a city break to the Berkley Hotel in Glasgow."

Dani's heart-rate sped up. "I wonder if Greta Bauer actually recalled ever having entered that competition?"

"If you've won a prize and the tickets drop onto your doormat, I don't suppose you're going to question it much."

Dani tapped her pen against the pad of paper containing the notes she'd made so far. "Can we assume Lomond deliberately lured the Bauers to that hotel room?"

"I'd say so, Ma'am. Have you had any luck yet in working out why he wanted them there?"

"No, there's nothing at all to suggest a connection. Denny is roughly the same age as the Bauers' children, maybe five years younger, but that's about it."

Sharon was quiet for a moment, before adding, "Dermot and I had a hunch Klaus Bauer got up to something top-secret when he worked for the GDR in the eighties. I've no idea if it has any bearing on Lomond's involvement, but we thought it could have put him under the spotlight of the Intelligence Services. Now Stefan is in possession of a letter which gives details of the work his father did behind the Iron Curtain. I'd love to see what was written there."

"I don't see how it would connect Klaus to Denny, but I agree it would make for fascinating reading. If the DCS allows us to overturn the Fiscal's finding of death by natural causes, we can probably instruct Stefan to release the letter to us."

Sharon sighed audibly. "I've spoken with the Fiscal's Office. The *PM* results still suggest natural cases for both Klaus and Greta. They say it doesn't much matter what position their bodies were in when they died, there's no forensic evidence to suggest a third party was involved. They didn't pick up any usable DNA from their nightwear - not anything that didn't belong to the Bauers themselves. I reckon the judgement will stand."

"Then it's up to us to find more evidence," Dani said resignedly.

"We'll get back on it first thing at this end. Good night, Ma'am."

"Good night, Sharon, and well done." Dani placed the phone back on the bed. Keating's painting was directly in her line of vision. She slid off the bed and turned it around, deciding to call it a night. Dani didn't fancy the image of the mangled, scorched plane being the first thing she set eyes on when she woke up.

*

Nate was looking excitable when Dani arrived at the criminal investigation department. He'd clearly had more luck than her.

"Dani, I've just got off the phone from the

Domestic Services Manager at Lomond Airlines." He pulled out a seat for her at his desk. "Diane Martin said he was efficient, and she wasn't wrong."

Dani raised her eyebrows with interest.

"I was requesting a full list of the names and addresses of their current cleaning and maintenance staff, when I had a thought. I decided to ask him for the details of anyone who had been employed at Lomond since they opened at Heathrow, three years ago. I thought maybe an ex-employee had held on to a uniform, or a pass perhaps? I know it happens here at the station sometimes."

"Good thinking." Dani gripped the arms of her chair.

"The manager was pleased to help. He had all the details on his database." Nate swivelled the screen 180 degrees. "Look who used to work at Lomond Airlines as a cleaner and maintenance man."

Dani blinked several times as she focused on the name. "John Lomond."

"Yep. He did the job for about six months in 2015. The manager said he was good at the maintenance stuff, but less good at the cleaning. He left to take on another job Mr Lomond had lined up for him, something with better prospects."

"Do we know what that was?"

"Supervising the renovation of Denny Lomond's property in Henley-on-Thames. John was the 'project manager', apparently, doing some of the building work himself."

Dani rubbed her brow. "John Lomond could easily still be in possession of a Lomond Airlines cleaner's uniform and entry pass. Is this enough for us to bring him in for questioning, along with the fact his build and height match the suspect in the CCTV?"

Nate grinned. "We'll face a shit-storm from the

Lomond lawyers, but I reckon it does, yes."

Chapter 34

The name of the place had firmly lodged itself in Rhodri's mind. Balloch House. It was the look Betsy had in her eyes when she implored her husband to take her back there that had stayed with him. Betsy claimed it was the only place she'd felt safe.

The plea reminded Rhodri of the words uttered by a handful of his own patients, the ones who became institutionalised during their treatment and feared the outside world. From the way Betsy spoke, he got the distinct impression Balloch House may have been a psychiatric unit. What in his early career would have been termed, an asylum.

There was no mention of the place in any of Betsy's psychiatric notes. Rhodri had gone online and put the name into a search engine. Balloch was a town in the Highlands, as he already knew. There was a castle there, plenty of hotels, but no Balloch *House*.

The professor drummed his fingers on the desk in his office. He couldn't shake the feeling Betsy's ramblings held some significance, they weren't the random nonsense that Mike suggested. Finally, Rhodri picked up his phone and dialled the number on the card in front of him.

"DI Muir? It's Rhodri Morgan, here. I'm sorry to bother you at work, but it's about Betsy Carlisle. I'm afraid her mental condition has deteriorated. I'd very much like a chance to discuss it with you further."

*

Sharon offered Rhodri a hot drink as soon as he stepped out of the lift onto the serious crime division office floor.

"No thank you, DS Moffett. But I appreciate the hospitality."

She led him straight to Bevan's office, where Dermot had the notes from the Bauer case laid out on the desk.

Rhodri raised his hand to wave to Andy Calder at his workstation as they passed. The DS was observing the arrival of the professor with an expression of confusion and disbelief.

"We've not had time to get Andy up to speed yet," Sharon said, by way of explanation. "I think he might actually explode."

"Oh dear, he doesn't like to be kept in the dark."

Sharon chuckled. "Let him stew."

The DS closed the door firmly behind them.

Dermot raised his gaze from the case file. "Good afternoon, Professor. I'm glad you could come in. I didn't want to explain all this over the phone." The DI gestured to the notes fanned out before them.

It took about thirty minutes to explain the latest developments in the Bauer case and how the German couple's deaths were linked to Bevan's investigation in London.

Rhodri lowered himself into a chair whilst he listened intently. "So, this Denny Lomond was Autumn's boss at Lomond Airlines, and he also owns the Berkley Hotel, where the Bauer couple were found dead?"

Dermot nodded. "Bevan thinks Denny Lomond lured the couple over to the hotel from Germany, then somehow orchestrated their deaths. Of course, he has an alibi for all the killings. But she's determined to make a connection between them."

"Is this Denny Lomond responsible for Autumn's death?"

"Again, he has a cast iron alibi for the night she died, but Bevan thinks he may get his brother, John, to perform the murders for him. The Hammersmith criminal investigation team are bringing him in for questioning today."

Rhodri shook his head in bewilderment. "Do you think Mike and Betsy could be connected to this in anyway? Is that why you wanted me to come here?"

Dermot shrugged. "There must be a reason why Autumn went to work for Lomond Airlines when she did. The interviews with her friends and ex-colleagues suggest she was happy at BA. She loathed the bucket-shop ethos of the budget airlines. Yet, she gave up everything to work for Denny Lomond. Within a couple of months, she was dead. We need to know what kind of hold he had over Autumn. Her parents may provide the key to understanding it. Perhaps Denny knew the family when he was in Glasgow?"

Rhodri rubbed his soft beard. "Betsy was muttering all kinds of stuff the other morning, when she was in a hyper-anxious state. She described an incident involving a vehicle crashing into trees. Betsy said she'd watched it happen from a window. The vehicle went on fire. Someone tried to release the driver from the wreckage, but they couldn't get near. She watched the man burn to death. Could that have been real?"

"Remember the transcripts of the nightmares Betsy suffered a few years ago. They were all about plane crashes. Could this vehicle she was talking about be an aeroplane?" Dermot eyed the professor carefully.

"It would certainly make sense. Aircraft are packed with fuel. If the tanks are ruptured in a crash, they very quickly go up in flames."

"Even if this event really happened, what has it got to do with Autumn Carlisle and Denny Lomond? Or the Bauers for that matter?" Sharon threw her arms up in the air.

Rhodri scratched his head vigorously, as if trying to encourage his brain to work harder. "The death of her daughter has unsettled Betsy's mental state. The words pouring out of her now could be the dislodging of memories long suppressed."

"Why would Betsy have needed to suppress them?" Dermot was staring fixedly at the professor.

"Because she was involved in something terribly traumatic, or illegal maybe. Betsy could have been keeping a secret to protect a loved one perhaps."

"We need more to go on than a sketchy description of an aircraft crash!" Dermot paced the room in exasperation.

"There *is* more." Rhodri shifted in his seat to keep Muir in his line of vision. "Betsy was begging her husband to take her to a place called *Balloch House*. Mike said it didn't exist, but I looked it up, anyway. I couldn't find a trace of any establishment of that name."

Dermot froze. "Balloch is near Inverness, isn't it? That's where Mike Carlisle grew up and spent his early career. It's where he and Betsy got married."

"Mike told me they'd lived for a while in the Highlands when Autumn was a small child. That could be where he meant."

"We need to find out where this Balloch House is, and what Betsy and Mike were doing there. If the place is real, then I think it will be the key to unlocking Betsy's memory."

Rhodri nodded solemnly. "I think you are right."

Chapter 35

Entering the interview room, Dani carefully took in the appearance of the man seated on the other side of the table.

John Lomond was like an elongated, broadened version of his older brother. Where Denny's hair had receded to nothing, John's was thick and dark, with only the most sporadic sprinkling of grey. But the family resemblance was still evident in the flat, boxer-like nose and deep-set eyes of the younger man.

The solicitor seated beside their suspect was impeccably dressed in a pin-striped jacket and silk blouse, a pair of designer glasses perched imperiously on the end of her nose.

Nate was reciting the time and date for the benefit of the tape recorder. He directed his gaze at Lomond. "John Lomond. Can you tell us how long you have resided at the Lake House, Henley-on-Thames?"

"Three years and two months." The reply was clipped and perfunctory.

"This property belongs to your brother, Dennis Lomond?"

"Aye, that's correct."

"Do you pay him any rent to live there?"

Lomond shifted in his chair. "I contribute to our household expenses, yes."

"How do you do that, Sir? We don't have any evidence that you are currently in employment?"

Lomond's eyes flashed irritation, anger maybe. "I keep the property maintained; tending the gardens and doing any work in the house that's needed.

When Denny bought the place, it required a total refurb. I took on a lot of the work myself. I did all the flooring and decorating."

"So, you are receiving a wage from Dennis Lomond?"

John sighed heavily. "Not as such. We're family. I help Denny out and he does the same for me. We don't have anyone else, just each other."

"But you have done paid work for Dennis Lomond's company in the past?" Nate make a point of flicking back through his notes. "You worked as a domestic cleaner and maintenance person for Lomond Airlines between February and July 2015, is that correct?"

John shot his solicitor a sideward glance. She nodded, almost imperceptibly. "Yes, that is correct."

"You would have been given a uniform and a security card during that time, so that you could move freely around the airport. What did you do with those items when you finished working for the airline in July 2015?" Nate leant forward. "Because the domestic services manager doesn't have any record of you returning them."

"I don't remember."

"Where were you on the afternoon of the 12th July, between four and six pm?"

"At home."

"Can anyone verify that's where you were?"

John shook his head. "I was working out in the garden. One of the neighbours might have seen me, or someone out on the river."

"And what about the night of the 3rd July, between midnight and 6am?"

"In bed, asleep."

"Do you know what happened on these dates?"

"Nope."

"Your brother's employees; Autumn Carlisle and

Kathy Brice were murdered."

He remained impassive, his gaze fixed on the table top.

"And what about the 28th of June? Were you in Henley on that date?"

John slid his eyes in the direction of his solicitor once again. This time she remained perfectly still. "No comment," he replied.

Nate slipped a piece of paper out of a plastic file. "I think you took a little trip on that date. We've found your name on the passenger list of a Lomond flight to Prestwick which arrived on the evening of the 27th. Where did you stay while you were in Glasgow? At one of your brother's hotels?"

John narrowed his eyes to pinpricks. "No comment."

"There's no record of you checking into either the Triton or the Berkley, but then, I don't suppose there would be. Your brother has his staff there very well trained to do what he asks. I'm sure they would happily give you a room, off the books. But taking a flight requires you to go through passport control, every individual is logged by airport security. There's no way to avoid leaving a trace. Perhaps you should have taken the car instead, eh?"

John clasped his hands together in his lap, as if holding himself back from placing them around Nate's throat.

"You see, the 28th June was the date when a German couple, called Mr and Mrs Bauer, died in a room in your brother's hotel. They'd both experienced a severe cardiac arrest. Although the manager tried to cover it up, we've discovered that they both appeared to have suffered a terrifying experience before death, one that no-doubt precipitated their heart attacks." Nate made a show of rummaging around in a bulky evidence bag by his feet. "We gained a warrant to search the house in Henley. Our team has been there all morning."

John's eyes were darting to and fro, but his body remained rigid.

"We didn't find the Lomond Airlines domestic cleaner uniform and lanyard, unfortunately." Nate gave an exaggerated frown. "But one of our officers did find this."

Lomond shot backwards in his seat as Nate brought a small bottle containing a metallic silver liquid out of the bag, placing it in the centre of the desk.

"It wasn't easy to find. It was under a floorboard in the boathouse by the river, where you keep your gardening equipment and tools. I don't suppose you could dispose of it as easily as a uniform and pass, not without poisoning half of west London in the process."

The solicitor cleared her throat. "What is it, exactly, Detective Inspector Lawrence?"

"Our forensic department reliably informs us this vial contains 25ml of mercury." Nate squinted at the container, as if in fascination. "Did you know, it's the only metal which is liquid at room temperature?" Nate reached out for the vial, swirling the liquid around inside it.

Lomond flinched. "Be careful, for Christ's sake," he hissed.

"Mercury is also known as quicksilver, because of its colour, I suppose. It was once widely used; in thermometers. That was before scientists discovered it was toxic to humans." Suddenly, Nate tossed the glass vial in the air, catching it again, just before it crashed to the floor.

Lomond kicked back his chair and leapt to his feet. "What the hell are you doing, you maniac?!" He glared at his solicitor. "He can't do that, can he? The man's going to bloody well poison us!"

The solicitor reached out to tug her client back into his seat. "Can we be spared the circus act, DI Lawrence. Please get to the point."

Nate grinned. "I see you understand the mercury's potentially toxic properties, Mr Lomond. The ancient Greeks thought it could prolong life. They put it into ointments and cosmetics. How wrong they were. We now know exactly what repeated exposure to mercury can do to a person." His expression grew more serious. "The chemical was used to make felt-hats in the 19th Century. Then all the workers started to display the psychological symptoms associated with mercury poisoning, hence the term, 'mad as a hatter'. They banned its use pretty much universally in the 1960s. I didn't know any of that until the techies told me. How about you, John. Did you know?"

The man grunted. His solicitor nudged his arm. "No comment," he managed to murmur.

"But it was still being used in the production of weapons, right up until the 1980s. It is still used in the production of nuclear bombs now. All the nastiest regimes and terrorists are trying to get hold of it."

John turned his gaze away from Lawrence. His mouth twisted into a grimace.

Nate held up the vial. "I don't really know why they would want it. Mercury can be so easily absorbed through the skin or through the nose and mouth as a vapour. If exposed over a series of time, a person can develop terrible side effects; it has a profound impact on the central nervous system, resulting in psychotic episodes. A sufferer of mercury poisoning will experience hallucinations and delirium, tremors, memory loss and even suicidal urges."

Dani was amazed to see John Lomond's mouth had drooped at both sides and his chin was trembling. Tears were escaping onto his cheeks.

Nate made his tone even, reasonable. "What were you doing with this bottle of mercury, John? Why was it hidden in your shed? It was a dangerous thing to keep on your property. What were you using it for?"

John wiped his sleeve across his face. "No comment," he croaked.

"I think we'd better take a break now," the solicitor said sternly.

Nate stood. "Sure, we'll continue after lunch." He signed off the interview and stopped the tape, placing the vial back into the evidence bag and leaving the room, with Dani close behind.

When they were safely out in the corridor, Dani lowered her voice, remarking, "is there really mercury in that container?"

Nate shook his head with a chuckle. "The vial they found in the boatshed is safely locked away at the forensic lab, awaiting confirmatory tests. This is one of the techie's test-tubes filled with silver car paint from Halfords."

Dani released a breath she didn't realise she'd been holding. "Thank God for that. Well, if you wanted to shake up Lomond, it certainly worked."

Nate shrugged. "We'll have to see. I don't know what upset him so much in there, or why he had that bottle of mercury stashed under the floorboards, but my gut tells me he used it to terrify the Bauers. The only question now is, *why*?"

Chapter 36

Rhodri had remained at the serious crime division for much of the afternoon. He and Sharon were accessing the archives of the land registry for the Inverness area, trying to find a property which had historically been known as Balloch House.

The professor had also spent an hour explaining the current situation to Andy Calder, who'd cornered Rhodri in the corridor when they finally surfaced from Bevan's office, refusing to let him pass until he 'spilled the beans' on what was happening.

Calder was now assisting them in their online searches. He was casting the occasional hostile glance at Sharon, whom he clearly felt should have involved him far sooner.

Dermot emerged from the office and approached them. "DCI Bevan has just been filling me in on the results of their interviews with Denny Lomond's brother. He's still not giving them much."

Sharon tutted loudly.

"But the DCI says they've got another problem. Denny Lomond didn't turn up for work at his offices in Heathrow this morning. The Met's team are still searching the premises and they spoke with his PA. She says Lomond had a packed schedule today, but he never arrived for his first meeting. She's been trying to reach him on his mobile but with no joy, it's clicking straight to voicemail. The Met are tracing the signal now to try and pinpoint a location for it."

"Has he done a runner?" Sharon got to her feet. "That's a fairly strong indicator of guilt."

"Yeah, but I'm surprised he'd leave his brother in police custody if he was going to do that. The boss made it sound like the men were really close." Dermot looked puzzled.

There wasn't time for the detectives to speculate any further on Denny Lomond's whereabouts. Rhodri's mobile phone began ringing in his pocket. The professor scrambled to answer it, noting the call was from Mike Carlisle. He quickly notched up the volume button. "Mike, how are things?"

The detectives gathered around to listen in to the conversation.

"I need your help, Rhodri!"

"Okay, try to stay calm. Tell me what's happened."

"It's Betsy, she's gone missing!"

"But I thought she was at the clinic in Kilsyth?"

"She was. Dr Acharya called me this morning. He said Betsy was much better. He wanted her to go home and recuperate. I think they needed her bed for a more chronic case who was coming in."

"Yes, that sounds reasonable. So, where is she?"

"I arrived at the clinic by lunchtime. Betsy was dressed and had her bags packed. We signed out and I helped her into the passenger seat of the car. Then she said she'd left her coat in the clinic. She said it was still on the bed in her room. Naturally, I went back inside to fetch it." He paused, there was a gulping sound, as if he was stifling a sob. "When I returned to the driveway the car was gone and so was Betsy. I ran down the road to see if I could follow her. There was no sign. I'd only been a couple of minutes. I don't know what to do, Rhodri!"

"Have you called the police? She is a very vulnerable person." The professor recognised the irony of his question, glancing at the three police officers surrounding him, following every word.

"Not yet. You are the first person I've told."

"Right, well, let me deal with the police. Tell me

exactly where you are. I'll be there as fast as I can."

*

Dermot drove the car, with Rhodri in the passenger seat. The DI had negotiated the city centre in quick time. They were now on the motorway, heading towards Kilsyth.

"Goodness, you're a very speedy driver, DI Muir. I feel like I'm in a police chase."

"I was an officer in the diplomatic division before coming to Pitt Street. I have an advanced license. Sometimes we needed to get the people we were protecting out of dangerous situations – fast."

"Well, it's certainly come in useful on this occasion."

"We'll be at the clinic in about ten minutes. The local traffic police have been alerted to be on the look out for Betsy and Mike's car." He sighed. "In reality, the woman is free to drive her own vehicle wherever she likes. The clinic had signed her off. She'd not had a sedative in over 12 hours. Dr Acharya didn't think she should have been there in the first place. He said Betsy's husband insisted they take her in and give her something to knock her out. It sounds like Betsy can make her own decisions. Maybe she's better off without Mike. It's certainly not really a police matter."

"I know, but only we understand the odd circumstances. If the Carlisles have a link to the four murders that have taken place, Betsy could be in real danger out there on her own; Mike or no Mike."

Muir nodded. He knew this was true.

The car finally pulled up onto the driveway of the clinic. Mike rose from a bench positioned at the edge of a pleasant front garden in full bloom, his face pinched into an anguished expression. Muir and Rhodri climbed out and approached him.

"Thank you for coming," Mike pronounced. "I'm

at my wits end. I couldn't go back inside, what would I tell them? The doctor thought he'd placed Betsy in safe hands."

Rhodri laid a hand on his friend's shoulder. "This is DI Muir, he's here to help us find Betsy. Did she have a mobile phone with her?"

Mike was ready to answer this. "Yes, but it will be switched off in her bag, she never uses it. Otherwise I would have tried to call it myself."

Muir shook his head. "We can't trace the phone unless it's switched on."

Rhodri made his tone firm but gentle. "Now, Mike, we need to know where Betsy might have gone to. She took the car over an hour ago. Time is running out to catch up with her."

Mike gazed down at his brown brogues. "I can't help you with that."

Rhodri shook his shoulder gently. "We've been friends for a long time, and I hope we trust one another. But in this instance, I must admit I don't believe you. I think you know exactly where Betsy has gone."

Mike wheezed, as if the air had been knocked out of his chest.

Rhodri persisted. "*Mike*, whatever you're hiding, it can't be worth this anguish. For God's sake, man. Your daughter is dead and your wife is missing! You need to tell us the truth!"

Mike took a step back, a stunned look on his face; as if he'd received a slap. "She will have gone to Inverness," he said bluntly. "Back to Balloch House."

Chapter 37

The journey to Inverness, even with Dermot's expert driving, was going to take over three hours. The DI had called ahead and notified the police station in Balloch that Betsy's car was headed in their direction. There were patrols out looking for her on all the roads in and out.

Mike was seated in the back. Dermot and Rhodri remained silent, allowing their passenger to speak, only interrupting if absolutely necessary. They didn't wish to disturb the flow of his story.

"I grew up in Inverness in the 1950s and 60s. I always had a natural ability with languages, so it was inevitable I would choose to read for a modern languages degree when I applied to Aberdeen University. I majored in German, but I am also fluent in French. I taught languages for my entire career." He turned to look out of the window, as the hills became higher and more rugged with every mile they travelled.

"It was at university that my interest in student politics was fostered. My father had always been left-wing, he was a great influence upon me. But at university I became friends with a group who introduced me to a more radical way of viewing the world. We studied the works of Marx and Engels; I in the original German. The ideological discussions about equality and community I read within those pages struck a chord with my young, radical self. Within a few months of being at college, I had joined the student communist society."

Rhodri raised an eyebrow, he hadn't known about his friend's radical past. He himself had been something of a hippie as a student, but Mike had always struck him as a more conservative type.

"We were at the height of the Cold War, yet our sympathies as a group lay with Russia. The capitalist and imperialist excesses of the USA held no appeal to me back then. I had a particular friend, a young man called, Jimmy, who claimed to have active connections with the Soviet Union." Mike sighed heavily. "I kept in touch with Jimmy even when I had graduated and become a teacher in Inverness. We'd been pals for twenty years when he contacted me about this *project* he needed help with."

"He and a group of his *associates* had taken over a run-down old country house near Balloch. They'd converted it into a type of residential hospital. Jimmy didn't tell me anything about the purpose of the place at first, just that they were looking after a group of patients who required intensive medical care. They also needed to learn decent language skills, and fast."

"And that's where you came in?" Rhodri commented, almost to himself.

"I was unsure at first. My job was respectable. I knew what Jimmy was asking me to do was going to be illegal, very possibly even *treasonous*. But I had no wife or family to worry about or put in jeopardy. I suppose I was looking for something to give purpose to my life."

"I recall the day I arrived so clearly. The house stood in its own grounds, surrounded by a forest of tall maples. The building was a little dilapidated, but inside, Jimmy and his friends had done a great job of making it pleasant and homely."

"My job was to teach the patients English. Most of them already knew a few words, some more, but I had to make them fluent; as accomplished in my mother tongue as if they'd been born and bred here in Scotland. Because the plan was that when they'd recovered sufficiently, they would stay in this country. Blend seamlessly into society with everybody else."

Rhodri twisted his body round to face the back seat. "These people would be spies for the Soviet Union?"

Mike's expression was sad. "I think that was the original idea. They would become *sleepers* in the UK, blending into the general population and being useful to the motherland when required. But this was the mid-eighties. The Cold War was thawing. Peace talks were reducing tensions between Russia and the west. Gorbachev had his *Glasnost* programme well underway."

"You referred to these people at the house as patients. What medical needs did they have?"

"The group I worked with had been technicians in a government weapons laboratory in east Berlin. They'd been constructing nuclear detonators. The use of the plutonium had been strictly controlled, but these women had routinely been exposed to mercury as part of the process."

"They were suffering from mercury poisoning?" Rhodri's mind was whirring fast. He knew a little about the effects of this particular chemical on the human nervous system; it caused hallucinations and psychotic episodes, deep depression and tremors in the body. He thought about Betsy's mental health issues over the years and the penny suddenly dropped.

Mike nodded, as if Rhodri had put voice to his thoughts. "For some it was more severe than for others. But they were well cared for by the medical volunteers. When they were well enough, I taught them English lessons in one of the downstairs drawing rooms. It had tall windows overlooking the lawn and was full of light. I visited the house at weekends and in my school holidays. The group made excellent progress."

"There was one student I bonded with more than the others. Her name was Elka. Her parents were from the Elbe Valley. She had excelled in science at school. The government in East Germany had recommended her for work in a prestigious armament laboratory in Berlin. Elka had worked there for ten years before she began to grow sick. Several other of her colleagues displayed similar symptoms."

"Why weren't they treated back in the GDR?" Rhodri asked.

"Because there was some sort of scandal about the way they'd been exposed to the mercury they were working with. The dangers of the chemical to humans was well-known by this time. The scientist in charge of the weapons programme was pushing his team too hard to get results. He cut corners with the safety procedures and exposed his technicians to the raw materials whilst keeping himself at a safe distance."

Dermot gripped the wheel more tightly, muttering under his breath, "Klaus Bauer."

"There was a sense within the East German government that when the grip of Soviet control loosened, there would be questions to answer about how these technicians had been allowed to become so sick. The recriminations would start. A new project was launched to deal with them. They would be smuggled into Scotland by Jimmy and his Soviet funded friends. They would treat the group, re-train them and turn them into Soviet informers within the country. The poor victims would be swallowed up within the strict rules of the KGB, their story a matter of national security."

"Did they all get better?" Rhodri knew prolonged exposure to mercury could be lethal.

Mike shook his head solemnly. "A couple died within the first few weeks of arrival. We buried their bodies in the grounds. Another woman, Elka's best friend, she seemed to have recovered well. But years later, she took her own life. We were lucky, Elka got off lightly by comparison with her symptoms. She'd not been as badly exposed as the others."

"After only a few months, Elka and I fell in love. We walked in the grounds of the house and shared our meals together. Jimmy encouraged our relationship, along with another of the patients who began seeing one of the doctors who volunteered there. He thought it would help them to integrate better into society when they left."

"Alongside the language classes, I also instructed the patients in Scottish history and culture. After about a year, they were ready to be given their new identities. Elka became Elizabeth. But I liked to call her Betsy, which had been my grandmother's name."

"When did the two of you marry?" Rhodri was fascinated by the idea of how this relationship had come into being.

"Jimmy drove us to the Town Hall in Inverness with a couple of his mates as witnesses, this was in 1987. His associates had produced a birth certificate for Betsy. It was the first proper test of the entire project; would the officials notice it was a forgery? But they never did. Betsy's accent and use of English were impeccable. I was a respectable local teacher. Our authenticity as a couple was never questioned. My parents thought we'd met through mutual friends. They considered Betsy a much-loved member of the family before they passed away."

Rhodri shook his head in amazement. He'd certainly never questioned their relationship in all the years he'd known them.

"I wanted to take Betsy home with me to my flat in the city, but the doctors at Balloch House said she wasn't well enough. She was still having nightmares and episodes of extreme anxiety. They let us have a set of rooms at the house, like a married-quarters. Betsy became pregnant in '88. The doctors were worried at first, but the pregnancy was a healthy one."

"You mean Autumn was *born* at Balloch House?" Rhodri's mouth fell open.

"Yes, in fact, motherhood seemed the best cure for Betsy. Autumn was born in the October, when the maple trees in the forest were ablaze with oranges and deep reds. It's the reason we gave her the name. She wasn't the only child at Balloch House either. Betsy's best friend Gretchen had arrived there from Germany with two children. One was only a baby and the other a toddler so they could not have been separated from her. Their father worked in a government department and remained in East Germany. I don't believe Gretchen ever saw him again. But her children were great company for Autumn during those three years we were at Balloch House. We were like a family in those early years, looking out for one another. Autumn played often with Gretchen's boys."

Dermot took his eyes off the road for a moment, twisting his head so his voice carried into the rear of the car. "What were the boys called?"

"Karl and Bruno," Mike replied, his tone devoid of any emotion.

"I don't think they are still called that now, Mr Carlisle. I'd stake my bloody career on the fact those little boys are now known as Dennis and John."

Chapter 38

The road sign that whipped past indicated it was only another fifteen miles until they reached the outskirts of Inverness. Soon, Dermot would need to rely on Mike to direct him to where they were going. The Sat Nav wouldn't be of any further use.

The occupants of the car had been silent for a short while. Each of the passengers absorbing the information they'd been told.

It was Mike who was the first to speak. "You think Dennis and John Lomond are Karl and Bruno? But why would they have hurt Autumn? The children were like brothers and sisters back then?"

Rhodri kept his tone soft. "It seems as if Dennis and John had discovered the identity of the scientist who exposed their mother, and Betsy, to the mercury when they worked for that weapons lab in the GDR. Do you recall a German couple who were found dead in a Glasgow hotel a few days before Autumn died?"

He nodded. "Yes, it was all over the news. But I tried to shield Betsy from the coverage. These depressing events have always upset her."

Dermot spoke up. "We discovered the man who died at the hotel in Glasgow, whose name was Klaus Bauer, had worked on a top-secret government project in east Berlin before the wall came down. He went on to have a well-regarded career as a biochemist in Frankfurt. I suspect Denny Lomond hired an investigator who found out much the same as us. He would have looked at the dates, perhaps matching the details with what his mother told him when she was still alive and decided Bauer was the culprit."

"The German man in the hotel was the scientist who poisoned Betsy?"

"I suspect so. We may even have a way of proving it. But I think Denny was fairly certain he was and was willing to act without any further proof." Dermot caught Mike's eye. "What exactly happened to Gretchen? Why would her sons be so set on revenge?"

Mike clasped his hands tightly in his lap. "When we were at Balloch House, she seemed to respond well to the treatment at first. I found her a very intelligent woman who had a natural gift for languages. She had her sons with her, which seemed to make her happier and more grounded than the other patients. But as time went on, her nervous symptoms worsened. Her hands trembled badly, and she hardly slept. Gretchen and the boys stayed at Balloch for longer than we did. I suppose that's why I never knew what new identities they were given. We weren't supposed to mix together on the outside, you see?"

"It was a wrench to part from them when we finally left. But Betsy and I bought a house in Inverness and lived there until Autumn started school, we quickly adapted to a normal life. Our daughter was about ten years old when we moved down to Glasgow. I got a job lecturing at the university. But I kept in touch with Jimmy. We spoke on the phone once a year. It was him who told me Gretchen was dead. Although she wasn't called that by then. It was about fifteen years ago. She'd stepped in front of a high-speed train. I never told Betsy, she wouldn't have been able to handle it. The damage to Gretchen's nerves from the mercury poisoning must have been too severe. We weren't able to save them all."

Rhodri turned to face his friend. "Why have you

never told me all this, Mike? Especially when Autumn died. It could have helped with the investigation. The Soviet Union collapsed in 1991, none of the group you coached can possibly now be considered *spies*. The Cold War is long gone. It's a piece of History."

Mike leant forward, his tone frantic. "The Cold War is over here in Britain, certainly. But as far as the Russian secret services are concerned, you are bound for life. Look what happened to the Skripals in Salisbury? Betsy and I signed a secrecy document for the KGB. We vowed never to speak a word about where Betsy had come from. I kept quiet for my wife's sake. If the FSB find out we've given information to the British authorities, we could both be killed!"

Dermot wondered if this was true, or just the paranoia of two people thoroughly brainwashed by Soviet agents thirty years ago.

"The only reason I told you now is because Betsy is in danger." Mike hung his head, cradling it in his hands. "I can only hope word doesn't get back to Moscow that I've talked. Ever since Autumn died, Betsy has been jabbering increasingly about the past. I've been terrified she'd let something slip. I made Dr Acharya sedate her because I needed her to stop her ranting and raving."

Rhodri turned back towards the road. He was beginning to question his friend's grip on reality.

"Right, we've reached the outskirts of Inverness. I'm relying on you now, Mike, to tell me where to go."

Mike raised his head, making an obvious effort to pull himself together. "You'll need to take the A96 towards Nairn, then make a right turn onto the road to Culloden."

Rhodri regarded the stunning scenery. He thought he could make out the mighty Cairngorm mountain range in the distance. But the light was rapidly fading, meaning he couldn't be sure.

Once they were off the dual carriageway, Mike's directions took them through a twisting sequence of country roads. Finally, Dermot swung the car onto a private lane which piloted them straight into a forest, dense with tall trees. The light was almost completely extinguished by the thick canopy of leaves towering overhead. Dermot flicked his lights to main beam which cut almost brutally through the darkness.

Mike visibly shuddered. "This is it."

They emerged onto a sweeping frontage which was banked by immaculate, emerald green lawns. The house itself was made of a silvery granite, the windows shiny and well maintained.

Mike looked at the lettering on a sign which was positioned at the roadside. "Well I never. It's now a hotel. I didn't know the old place could be made to look so good."

Dermot felt a tightness in his chest. His uneasiness was growing. The sign he'd just read didn't augur well for poor Betsy. The hotel was called, The Highlander. The smaller script below informed him it was a part of The Lomond Group.

There were few spaces free in the car-park at the rear of the building. The men scoured the lines of vehicles for the Carlisles' Hyundai. There it was. Parked under one of the huge trees.

Mike released the car door before Muir had the chance to secure the hand break, running over to the little hatchback with an agility that belied his age. He immediately checked the interior and boot. "Her bags have been taken out. She must have gone inside."

Dermot caught up, resting his hand on the man's arm. "We need to take this slowly, Mike. I think we should wait for back-up before we go any further."

He creased his face in disbelief. "But it's been hours already since Betsy took off. There's no more time to lose!"

Rhodri spoke to his friend in a level, reasonable tone. "This house is now one of Denny Lomond's hotels. DCI Bevan told us earlier that the man can't be traced, he's no longer in London. Do you know what this might mean?"

Mike gasped. "He might be in there with Betsy! The man who was involved in Autumn's death!"

Dermot intervened. "We cannot be certain of that. I think we need to remain calm."

As they were having this discussion, Mike abruptly turned his face towards the house. He stared up at a window in the top floor, under the jutting eaves of the roof. "That's her! She's at the window!" He began waving wildly. "I'm coming, my darling. Wait there!"

Before Dermot could do anything, Mike had made a dash for a pair of French doors at the back of the hotel. He and Rhodri set off on his heels.

They entered a ground floor room which had the appearance of a residents' lounge. A large fireplace was flanked by cherry wood bookcases and framed prints of horses.

Mike had already navigated the chintzy furniture and emerged into the hotel's lobby. A woman in a tartan jacket and thick make-up stepped out from behind a solid oak desk.

"Can I help you, Sir? Do you want to check in?"

"I'm looking for my wife. She arrived a few hours ago. Her name is Betsy Carlisle."

The woman calmly returned to her computer screen. She tapped away on a keypad for far longer than was necessary.

Mike was looking around him frantically. Dermot

and Rhodri stood by his side.

She shook her static hair and gave them a look of exaggerated mock sympathy. "I'm terribly sorry, Sir. Your wife has not checked in today. Perhaps she's having a coffee in the Culloden Bar, just along the corridor, there? I expect she was waiting for you to arrive first."

Mike released a grunt of exasperation. "I just saw her upstairs, through the window!"

Before the woman could respond, Mike was bounding up the sweeping staircase.

"You can't go up there, Sir! Not without having a room booked!"

Dermot brought out his warrant card, which he flashed at the receptionist by way of explanation before following the man up the stairs.

The DI took them two at a time, with Rhodri trailing behind. "Don't lose him," the professor puffed. "He's the only one who knows where he's going."

Mike was quicker on his feet that the others would have predicted. He kept spiralling upwards until the staircase halted at a landing with a balcony. Mike only hesitated for a couple of seconds before turning left, wrenching open a fire-door and disappearing beyond.

Dermot was close enough behind to see where the man was heading. The DI could tell this wasn't a residential part of the hotel. The corridor beyond the fire-door was narrow and cheaply carpeted. The rooms weren't furnished with the key insert lock mechanisms you'd expect in an establishment of this calibre.

Mike was nowhere to be seen.

"Damn," Dermot muttered under his breath. He stalked the corridor quietly, listening for any sound. Finally, when he was about half way along, he heard a deep voice resonating behind one of the doors. He then discerned a high-pitched yelp, which he assumed must be Betsy.

He knew the protocol was to await the back-up team which was currently heading towards their location from Inverness, but Dermot also knew Mike and Betsy were in danger. He could hear an unfamiliar man's voice rumbling within the room.

The Carlisles were most definitely not alone.

Chapter 39

Mike burst into the room, closing the door behind him. Betsy was seated on the edge of a single bed which was made up with plain, white cotton sheets. She exclaimed at his sudden arrival. Her bags were placed neatly under the small window in the eaves.

"Betsy, thank goodness. Are you okay?"

She opened her mouth to reply. Before she could utter a word, a squat, bald man stepped out of the en-suite bathroom.

"Ah, Mike. I thought you might turn up sooner or later." Denny Lomond glanced over the shoulder of their visitor. "Are you alone?"

Instinct told Mike to avoid informing this man of Dermot and Rhodri's presence in the building. "Of course I am. I've come to take my wife home. I'd hardly let the police know about this place."

Denny smiled. "I don't think Betsy wants to leave just yet, do you? She was perfectly happy to come and join me here when I called her. Happy even."

Mike gave his wife a puzzled look. "Betsy?"

"Well, *you* wouldn't agree to bring me back here, even when I begged you to." She gazed up at Lomond, a dreamy expression on her face. "Don't you recognise him? It's Karl. Gretchen's boy."

Mike felt his blood run cold. "Yes, I do recognise him."

"What's the matter, Mike? I thought you'd enjoy a nice reunion? This is the room that Betsy had when she was a patient here, do you remember that? The views out over the forest are stunning. Mum, Bruno and I were just two rooms down. It was rather cosy, wasn't it?"

"Where is your mum now?" Betsy asked innocently. "I'd love to see her again." Her eyes misted over with tears.

Denny leant down and took her hands. "She passed away, I'm afraid. A long time back now."

The tears escaped, sliding down Betsy's cheeks. "I'm so sorry. I wish I'd known."

"I'm surprised you didn't. It was all over the news. Jimmy knew about it. He came to pay his respects." Denny flashed Mike an accusing look. "You could have come to the funeral if *someone* had told you."

Mike felt the anger surge up inside him, settling in his throat like a knot. "What did you do to Autumn?"

Betsy looked across at her husband, confusion clouding her features. "What are you talking about?"

He reached out and grabbed Denny by the arm, dragging him to his feet. "*He* knows! What did you and your thug of a brother do to our little girl?"

Denny shook him off. "You shouldn't have done that, old man. I'm sorry about Autumn. I thought she'd want to help us, but she didn't appreciate our methods."

Mike narrowed his eyes. "She would never have countenanced *murder*."

"No, I misjudged her on that score. I'd followed her career for years. I wasn't ever likely to forget that name, and those flaming red locks. She'd been a sister to Bruno and I. That's why I thought she'd help."

"You wanted revenge against Klaus Bauer."

Realisation was beginning to dawn on Betsy. "Professor Bauer. We worked for him in Berlin."

Denny turned towards her. "And he poisoned you in the process. You and all the others, including my mother." He scratched irritably at the side of his face, Mike noticed he'd drawn blood. "You never suffered like she did. Mum used to cry out at night, terrified by the dreams and hallucinations. We had to hold her until she eventually went back to sleep. It was like Bauer had sentenced her to a living torture. No wonder she was so desperate to end the torment that she allowed herself to be shredded to pieces on a train track." He looked at Mike with feverish, red-rimmed eyes. "There was barely enough left of her for Bruno and me to bury, did you know that?"

"I tried to help Gretchen. We all did. Autumn was innocent, a victim just like you, why hurt her, *why*?"

Denny walked over to the small window, gazing out over the grounds, now blanketed by darkness, a starless night. "I didn't want to. I sought Autumn out over a year ago. We met a few times at her cottage in East Sussex, we drank at the pub together. I wasn't sure if she would remember us, but she did, just about. I spent hours persuading her we needed to bring Bauer to justice. It had taken me two years of private detective work to track him down. Now I had a plan. But I needed Autumn to get close to the family, to gain their trust, so I could inflict the same horror on them that they'd inflicted on us. I wanted to infect their whole family with mercury, even the grandchildren. But I needed to gain access to their home, to put it in the water system perhaps. I was going to get Autumn to crew the flights to Frankfurt, infiltrate their lives over several months. Whatever it took."

Mike shook his head. "Autumn wouldn't have gone along with it. We brought her up to be kind, law-abiding."

"That was the problem." He sighed heavily. "Autumn came to work with me at Lomond Airlines after I told her the full story of how Klaus Bauer's negligence had ruined the lives of both our mothers. When she knew, she was determined to help me bring Bauer to justice. But Autumn wanted it to be legal. She wanted us to find evidence to bring him to trial – back in his native Germany she hoped."

"You had other plans."

Betsy was listening to these words in growing horror. "What are you saying, Karl?"

"If my wife Kelly was still alive and I still had something to live for, I might have gone along with Autumn's plan. To be honest, I was tempted for a while. We spent a lot of time together and I remembered how close we were back here. How we only had each other. But Bruno wasn't happy with how things were going. It was him who'd tracked Autumn down for me. He'd been watching her for years, following her, keeping tabs on her. He thought he was doing me a favour. In reality, I think he was obsessed."

Betsy placed her hands over her ears. "I don't want to hear it!"

"Bruno got tired of waiting. He persuaded me it was time to take action. We'd been talking about it for too long. He thought Bauer might cark it before we ever got our revenge. So, we came up with the idea of the online competition. It was remarkably easy to set up. Within a couple of weeks, the Bauers were safely installed in one of my own hotels."

"In Glasgow?"

"That's right. At least one of us needed to have an alibi, so I sent Bruno. He'd got hold of a bottle of mercury on the dark net, had it sent direct to the Berkley. There's no way he would've got that through security and onto a plane." Denny laughed.

"What the hell was he planning to do with it? Hasn't that stuff done enough damage?" Mike had sidled across the room to sit on the bed beside his wife, taking her hand.

"Bruno got a key to their room from the manager, who does anything I ask him to. My brother sat on the end of their bed until the sound of his breathing must have woken them up. He wanted to savour every moment. They were terrified. You'll be gratified to know that Bruno made them suffer. He told them exactly what Klaus's negligence and arrogance had resulted in. Then he got out the vial. He told them he was going to pour it down their throats, then he was going to track down every single member of their family and do the same to them. I'm sure he had every intention of doing just that, but suddenly Klaus started gasping and clutching at his chest. He died in minutes. His wife was curled up in a ball on the bed, whimpering. Bruno left her there. He warned her not to move until morning or he'd come back in and kill her, too. It seems the shock stopped her heart some time later, because by morning, she was dead, alongside her husband. Fortunate, really. Bruno never even had to touch them."

Betsy was dry retching. "How did that help anyone?"

Denny chuckled. "That's exactly what your daughter said, when she found out. She read about the couple's death on the news. She knew I was somehow behind it. We argued about it at work. Autumn said she was going to the police. Well, we couldn't have that, could we?"

Mike leapt up and grabbed for him. "You didn't have to kill her, you bastard!"

Denny shoved him to the ground. "Actually, Mike. I'm inclined to agree. I was preparing to talk Autumn around. It wasn't like we'd strangled the old pair with our bare hands. It would have been tough for the police to make a cast-iron case against us. But Bruno took the initiative onto himself. He'd already been casing out her flat. He knew a way in through the old dear's place on the floor below. She always left her kitchen window open. The silly bint had Autumn's key in a pot by the front door. In fact, he'd used it to slip in there before. He liked to watch her sleeping."

Mike used all his energy to make a further grab for Denny. The younger man was too quick for him; he sidestepped towards the wall, allowing Mike to crash painfully onto the bedside table. The older man cried out in agony.

"But this isn't why we're here," Denny continued, in a reasonable tone. "I wanted to offer you this room back, Betsy. I remembered how much you loved it. I'm sorry about Autumn, I swear I am. But perhaps now I can make amends. I bought the house as soon as I could gather together the funds. I wanted us all to be able to come back here again. It's our home. Bruno will join us as soon as my lawyers get him released."

Betsy shook her head in disbelief. "You killed our daughter and scared an old couple to death. This isn't what Gretchen would have wanted."

"We were always family. Mum would have wanted us to be together now. It's what I've been working all these years for."

Betsy bent down and cradled Mike in her arms. "You disgust me," she spat over her shoulder. "I don't recognise the monster you've become."

Denny didn't have time to answer. The door to the room burst open. Within seconds, the cramped space was filled with police.

Chapter 40

"A very fine set-up you've got here." Nate Lawrence followed Dani across the floor of the serious crime unit at Pitt Street, Glasgow.

The DI from the Met shook hands with Dermot Muir when they reached the threshold of Dani's office.

"Great work bringing in Denny Lomond," Nate said with genuine admiration.

Dermot creased his brow. "It was very much a team effort. If Mike Carlisle hadn't contacted Professor Morgan and told him where Betsy was heading, we'd be none the wiser."

"Yes, but it was you and DS Moffett who kept digging into the Bauer deaths. You had the collective instinct to know there was more to that situation than met the eye."

"How is Mike Carlisle?" Dani asked.

Dermot grimaced this time. "He's at Raigmore Hospital with a cracked rib. Betsy is by his side. I feel terrible. I heard a crash inside the room, but I didn't go in immediately. It's my fault Mike's in hospital."

"You made a judgement call. You were recording what you could of Denny's confession on your phone through the door. The Carlisles will just be pleased when we manage to secure a conviction for their daughter's murder."

Sharon brought over a tray of coffees.

"Thank you, Sharon," Dani said gratefully. "Please stay and join in the debrief. You've played as much of a part in this as the rest of us."

The DS scooped up a mug and leant her weight

on a nearby desk. "Thank you, Ma'am."

"What is happening with John Lomond?" Dermot enquired.

Nate answered, "he's still in custody at my station in west London. We've charged him with the murder of Autumn Carlisle, based on Denny's confession which we have recorded, and Mike and Betsy's sworn testimony. Lomond's lawyers failed to get him granted bail."

"The Met are still gathering evidence in relation to the murder of Kathy Brice. Now we know John had access to a cleaner's uniform and security pass plus the CCTV image which matches his height and build, he remains the main suspect," Dani explained.

"We think Kathy Brice overheard a conversation between Denny and Autumn about their plans for the Bauers. She thought they were having an affair and had been watching their movements closely. When we brought Denny's secretary in for questioning at the station, she admitted that Kathy had gossiped to her in the canteen about hearing some type of altercation between the CEO and Autumn. Kathy hinted that what she heard was very damaging for them both. Diane Martin mentioned this to Denny. She's extremely loyal to her boss."

Sharon tutted. "So, Kathy's gossiping got her killed?"

"It's what we suspected all along," Dani explained. "Kathy had hated Autumn ever since she'd got promoted ahead of her. Kathy was waiting to gather evidence against her crew manager by eavesdropping into her conversations. If Denny thought Kathy knew about his involvement in the deaths of the Bauers, she was a big danger to him."

"Kathy had been talking to us the morning of the day she died," Nate said solemnly. "Lomond must have panicked."

"I think Denny called Kathy during one of the toilet breaks from his meeting with the union bosses. He told her to go to gate 52. Perhaps he said a passenger had been taken ill in the ladies' loos and they needed a representative from Lomond Airlines to help sort it out," Dani continued.

"Whatever reason he gave, Denny was the boss and Kathy wouldn't have questioned it." Nate sighed heavily. "When the poor woman got down there, John was waiting for her."

Dermot took a gulp of coffee. "I read the report. John strangled her, probably with his belt and left her body in one of the cubicles." He shook his head. "Denny's brother sounds like a nasty piece of work."

"It seems John had been following Autumn on and off for years. She must have noticed. It would have been terrifying. I get the sense he enjoyed killing her. It was a pleasure for him."

"Perhaps the mercury poisoning somehow affected how he turned out," Sharon added thoughtfully. "His mother must have had the chemical surging through her system when she was pregnant with him. Maybe that's why he's turned out so wrong?"

Dani shrugged. "It's definitely a possibility. I don't know enough about the effects of the chemical to be able to hazard a guess. Rhodri might have an opinion on it."

"I've written to Stefan and Mila Bauer," Sharon went on. "I told them of John Lomond's presence in their parents hotel room the night they died. I've also requested a copy of the letter Stefan was sent by one of his father's work colleagues in Berlin. Perhaps the contents of that will finally prove whether or not Klaus was guilty of poisoning all those people."

Dermot's expression was sombre. "I don't think

we'll be able to prosecute John or Denny Lomond in relation to the deaths of the Bauers. We've got Denny in the cells downstairs awaiting questioning in relation to it, but I think breaking and entering and intimidation are the best we'll manage."

"It's not a great result for Stefan and Mila," Sharon added.

"Which is why it's important to focus now on the murders of Kathy and Autumn. With Denny's confession and the evidence tying Lomond to the scene of at least one of the killings, I remain hopeful," Dani said.

Dermot drained his mug. "What about Mike and Betsy? Now we know they were involved with the Soviet Union, potentially as spies against Britain, what will happen to them?"

Dani shook her head softly. "We pass the details onto the intelligence services. It will be in their hands then. They will decide what to do."

"Might Betsy be sent back to Germany?" Sharon asked.

"She's married to a British citizen so I wouldn't have thought so," Nate stated. "The Cold War ended a long old time ago. I don't expect anyone will consider them a threat now."

"The intelligence services will probably want to question Mike about his associates back in the 1980s. It definitely sounded like this Jimmy character was a Soviet Agent. But whether Mike and Betsy will face charges is another matter. I think they were more afraid of retribution from Moscow than the authorities here, for breaking their cover." Dermot crossed his arms over his chest.

Dani let out a humourless grunt. "I wonder how many other sleepers are out there, still believing they are working for the Russians?"

Nate put down his mug with a flourish. "Happily,

that's not our concern. I'm just looking forward to questioning Denny Lomond again. I want to see his face when he realises we've got his confession on tape."

"Can I sit in on the interview, Ma'am?" Dermot asked expectantly.

"Of course," Dani replied. "You've performed outstandingly in this investigation." She ushered him in the direction of the lifts. "I was rather hoping we could have a talk about maybe extending your contract?"

"That's certainly a possibility, Ma'am."

Chapter 41

Before reaching Raigmore Hospital in Inverness, Rhodri had driven Dani on a detour. He bumped his car along the private drive which led to The Highlander hotel. The sun was high in the sky and the landscape bathed in golden light.

Dani observed the forest of maple and pines which surrounded the house. The tall boughs put her in mind of the line of trees which flanked Autumn's cottage in Mitchling. It seemed clear now, that they reminded her of the time she'd spent here in the Highlands during the early years of her life.

Rhodri didn't stop. He swept the car around and headed back towards the city. Neither felt a desire to linger in the place.

Rhodri had brought a potted plant and a basket of fruit. Dani had her own offering, wrapped in brown paper and tucked under her arm.

Mike had a bed on one of the general wards. As they approached it, Betsy was arranging some pretty carnations in a vase.

Rhodri was the first to speak. "How are you feeling, Mike? I hope they're treating you well?"

The man automatically put a hand to the bandage wrapped around his chest, just visible through the gaps between the buttons of his striped pyjamas. "I'm a bit sore, but I'll live. They're releasing me tomorrow, which is just as well, as the poor neighbours have got Dodie."

Dani creased her brow in puzzlement.

"The dog," Rhodri explained to her.

"I just hope they're keeping her well away from that rabbit," Betsy commented.

Rhodri couldn't help but smile. His friends seemed to be getting back to normal.

Dani cleared her throat. "John Lomond has been charged with your daughter's murder. After forensic tests were carried out, traces of Autumn's blood were found in the treads of a pair of his black work shoes. The techies are also pretty sure they match the scuff mark I found in her bedroom at the flat in Hillingdon."

Betsy sighed. "Little Bruno. Who would have imagined it?"

"What about Denny Lomond?" Mike asked, a hint of anger in his voice.

"Well, he will be charged with actual bodily harm in relation to the assault on you. We also hope to secure a conviction for two counts of accessory to murder, although this isn't as foregone a conclusion as John's conviction." Dani wanted to be as honest as possible with the couple.

Mike grunted. "I hope he doesn't get away with it."

Dani didn't reply. She couldn't make any false promises. Suddenly, she recalled the package down by her feet. "Mr and Mrs Carlisle, when I was down in Sussex, I recovered some artwork which belonged to your daughter. I thought you might like one of the paintings."

"Autumn was very keen on her art, wasn't she Mike? She had friends in Amsterdam who made the most wonderful wooden sculptures of animals. We've got one in our garden that she brought back for us."

"This piece seemed to mean a lot to Autumn. She visited the artist to get the story behind it. Rhodri thinks you may know why she was so interested in the subject matter." Dani ripped off the brown paper and showed Arthur Keating's watercolour to Betsy.

She immediately threw a hand up to cover her

mouth. "It's the plane crash!"

Rhodri edged forward in his chair. "What plane crash, Betsy?"

Betsy glanced at her husband, as if gaining permission to speak. He gave a curt nod.

"It happened in the winter of 1990. We had been given a couple of rooms on the top floor of Balloch House as our family quarters. Autumn was a toddler. She was asleep in her little bed in the adjoining room. Or I always thought she was."

"At first, all I heard was the persistent buzzing of an engine circling overhead. Then it started to falter. I had the feeling something was terribly wrong. Mike was downstairs somewhere. I went to the window, the one which looked out over the woods."

"It was night by this time. All I could see was a single light, holding quite still over the trees, like an eye in the dark. I couldn't hear the engine at all by this point. The plane must have lost power and was gliding towards the huge maples because then there was a terrible crack, like thunder in a storm as the plane hit the branches and plummeted to the ground."

"Jimmy and I heard the noise and ran out to see what was happening," Mike explained. "We approached the wreckage with flashlights. The plane had become lodged in a gap between the trunks of two of the largest maples. The pilot was slumped over the controls. We thought he'd probably died on impact. Then, he suddenly raised his head."

"I saw all this from the window," Betsy continued. "Jimmy tried to wrench open the door to the cockpit with a branch. When that didn't work, he hammered on the windscreen. But by this point, I'd seen the flames licking the back of the plane. Within seconds, the wreckage was engulfed."

Mike shook his head sadly. "Jimmy tried his best.

His hands were burnt from his efforts to free the pilot. The fire took hold too quickly. Then the fuel tank exploded."

Betsy put her head in her hands. "I saw the man's face in that final moment. I'll never forget the look in his eyes."

"Others had joined us by this point. We tried to contain the fire as best we could. But the ground was damp. The inferno burnt itself out pretty quickly without our help."

"What about the pilot? People must have been searching for him?" Dani was transfixed by the tale and appalled in equal measure.

"Oh yes, they were. His name was Alec Docherty. He had a wife and two children. He'd been flying his light aircraft out of an airfield near Nairn. The papers were full of the search for weeks. Some experts suggested he may have hit one of the mountains in the Cairngorms, the wreckage being covered by a heavy fall of snow, others that he went down over the North Sea. The area covered by the recovery teams was vast."

"But *you* knew exactly where he was. Why didn't you notify the authorities?" Rhodri couldn't hide his shock.

"Because our project at Balloch House was top secret. If the police had come poking around, it would all have been over." Mike swallowed, as if his mouth was dry. "As soon as the wreckage cooled, we pulled his body out. We gave him a decent burial. Then set about getting rid of the wreckage. We buried sections of it and used some of the metal to make railings for the house. Over time, the trees recovered from the fire and the branches grew to cover the crash site."

"I'm going to need you to show me where his body is buried," Dani said gently. "His family will want to know."

Mike nodded. "Yes. We marked it with a small cross. Hopefully it's still there."

Betsy stared at the painting. "How did Autumn have a picture of what happened? I don't understand?"

"This is a painting by a man called Arthur Keating. He witnessed a light aircraft crash similar to the one you did. In this case, the pilot was pulled out alive. Autumn saw this painting and was drawn to its subject matter. She even contacted Keating and visited the site of the crash, in woods behind his house." Dani cradled the picture in her arms.

"I thought Autumn slept through it all. She must have been woken by the noise and gone to the window next door." Betsy choked back a sob. "I never knew she'd witnessed it too."

"I don't think she did either," Rhodri said. "She was only two years old. The event must have lodged itself in her subconscious somewhere. The fascination with planes, with flying, was clearly a manifestation of this early experience. But when Denny approached your daughter and began talking to her about their time at Balloch House, I think it released this suppressed trauma."

"Was that why she was having those nightmares?" Mike asked.

"I think so. Autumn was drawn to that painting because it reproduced a scene from her early childhood. She was finally starting to process the horror she'd seen. With time, I'm sure she would have dealt with it and put it to rest."

Betsy was weeping quietly.

"Will we be charged?" Mike asked bluntly. "For hiding the pilot's body and disposing of the wreckage?"

Dani shook her head. "I genuinely don't know.

Much will depend on what his surviving family want."

Mike nodded in resignation.

Rhodri got to his feet. "We'll leave you now. Do try to get some rest, Mike."

*

It wasn't until they had emerged into the bright sunshine of the car-park that either of them said anything.

"I don't think there's going to be a happy ending for the Carlisles." Dani opened the passenger door and climbed inside.

Rhodri ducked in beside her. "No, there isn't. Mike and Betsy have been party to too many lies. Whatever their motives in covering up that crash, it is inexcusable."

Dani sighed. "Sending that pair to prison doesn't feel like it will achieve much."

"Just focus on the fact you caught Denny and John Lomond. They are the real villains in all of this."

Dani gazed out of the window as Rhodri pulled away from the hospital grounds, pointing them in the direction of home.

She thought about the boys' mother; her sickness and the brutality of her suicide. Karl and Bruno's abandonment by their father and the fact that both could have been suffering the effects of mercury poisoning themselves. It made her wonder if Rhodri's words were true at all.

*

© Katherine Pathak. All rights reserved, 2019© The Garansay Press. All rights reserved, 2019

If you enjoyed this novel, please take a few moments to write a brief review. Reviews really help to introduce new readers to my books and this allows me to keep on writing.
Many thanks,

Katherine.

If you would like to find out more about my books and read my reviews and articles then please visit my blog, TheRetroReview at:

www.KatherinePathak.wordpress.com

To find out about new releases and special offers follow me on Twitter:

@KatherinePathak

Printed in Great Britain
by Amazon